BETH BALL

PROMISE

Published by Grove Guardian Press

Edited by The Blue Garret

Cover design by Mibl Art

Paperback ISBN 978-1-952609-37-4

Ebook ISBN 978-1-952609-38-1

groveguardianpress.com

ALSO BY BETH BALL

Heir of Lilith

Phantom

Pain (forthcoming)

Age of Azuria

Buried Heroes

Hadvarian Heist

Amber Queen

Forest Deep

Shadows Beneath

Feather & Flame

Phoenix Rising

Novellas and Short Stories

Promise, an *Heir of Lilith* novella

Aurora, an *Age of Azuria* novella

Song of Parting, an *Age of Azuria* novella

Story Magic, an *Age of Azuria* novella

Stormborn, a standalone *Tree of Silver* novella

"Blood Wolf Moon" an *Age of Azuria* story

"The Shadow's Embrace" an *Age of Azuria* story

"Nocturne" an *Age of Azuria* story

To my sisters
Who have fought by my side from the beginning

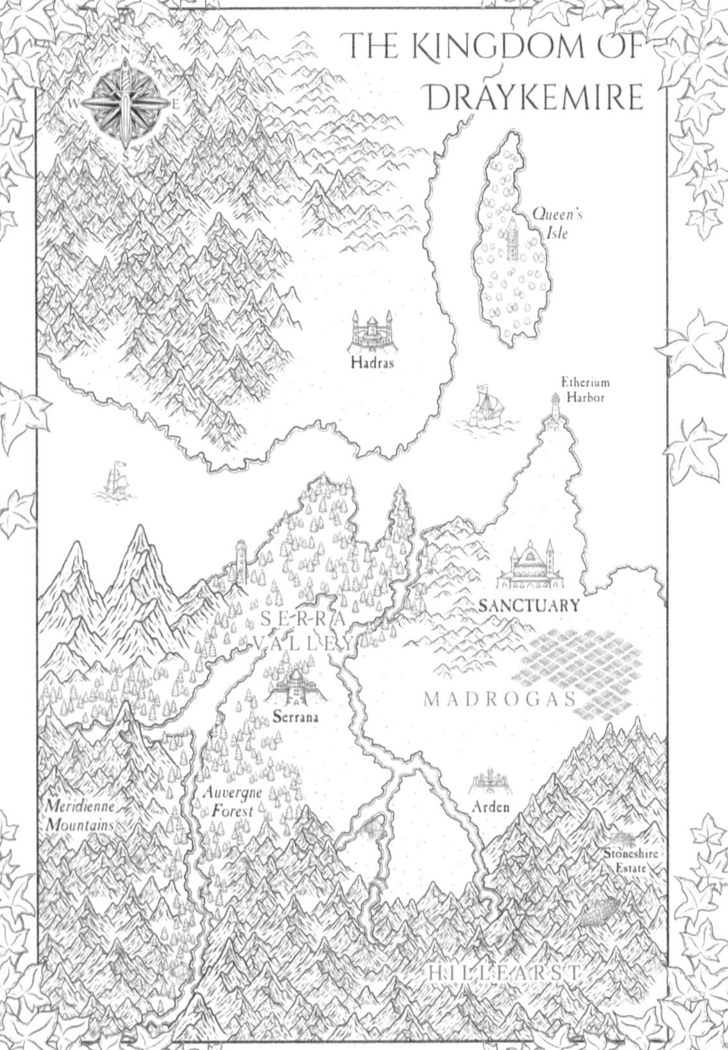

THE KINGDOM OF DRAYKEMIRE
Queen's Isle
Hadras
Etherium Harbor
SANCTUARY
MADROGAS
SERRA VALLEY
Serrana
Auvergne Forest
Meridienne Mountains
Arden
Stoneshire Estate
HILLEARST

DUR'FOR
HALLOWED HILLS
BASTI
VERITA
THE GLADE OF SHADOWS
SCOURGE

NORTHLANDS
FAER HAVEN
VESTIGE
DRAYKEMIRE
MERIDIENNE MOUNTAINS
RESPITE
IS-MAEN
RAL
THE GREEN MOUNTAINS
THE EMERAUDE
PALAIS
BEACON
THE WORLD OF ELDURA

Pain and blood mark the path to Vengeance.

CHAPTER 1

NATALYA

Natalya tore through the nobles' district of Serrana, dodging servants struggling behind carefully wrapped packages, darting past drivers whose gaudy livery cost more gold than she'd ever seen through the first fifteen years of her life, and barreling straight through a gaggle of priestesses in flowing emerald gowns. The priestesses' titters of disapproval still echoed above the din of the street behind her as she pounded on the iron gate of Lord Atkinson's manor house at the far edge of the district, just bordering the merchants' quarter.

Had the need been less dire, she would have traveled along the docks, her brilliantly white hair and pointed fae ears covered so she might pass unrecognized. She was a known entity among Serrana's sailors and thugs; the backing of Randolf, the Tidings, and her own reputation usually secured her exactly what she wanted without having to gut anyone with one of her magic blades.

An elderly gate attendant wobbled toward her. Was the man moving through sludge?

Natalya clenched her fists against her stomach, willing the blades to stay hidden. An armed display would not grant her ready entry to the lord's estate any more than charging through the nobles' district beneath a hood would result in faster passage between their stately homes—it resulted only in a lock-up in the city's prisons, and she wouldn't endure Randolf's mockery at having to bail her out of there again.

"My sister called for me," Natalya hurriedly told the ambling attendant. "I think she's in trouble."

"Wh-what sister would that be?" He moved at such a sluggish pace and spoke even more slowly, Natalya couldn't tell if he'd registered her Shadowlands accent or if he simply struggled to speak and walk at the same time.

"Piper." Her voice quavered, the nerves that had sped her flight here jumbling up now that she'd met her first obstacle. "I mean—Miss Slipshayde." The nobles and courtiers were rather particular about their titles. This glacially paced attendant might not know Piper by her first name. Natalya rolled up onto her toes, trying not to openly bounce upon them. She glanced up at the pointed iron tips of the gate, barbed teeth meant to deter bandits.

Such protections had never stopped her before, but she wouldn't risk further harm to Piper's tenuous position within her new Suzerain's house by scaling the gate and bolting past this man who was clearly incapable of catching her.

"The courtesan who moved here not eight weeks ago," Natalya added, hoping that citing her sister's position within the city might help to offset the rough-spun marks of her own garb.

"O-oh, yes. The pretty fae." The elderly attendant nodded his approval at his lord's choice. "She looks different than you."

Natalya exhaled her impatience. Piper's dark hair, coppery skin, and copper-red eyes contrasted sharply with her own pale complexion, but she didn't have time for such inane observations. "I need to see her," she insisted.

"Alright, alright, young miss. Let me just check the ledger . . ." He made to slowly turn about to consult the list he'd received from the main house.

"Please—" Natalya dropped her voice an octave, not bothering to hide the warning tone, the note that sent a chill down sailors' spines as they attempted to unload their wares in the middle of the night, as though the moons wouldn't betray them. As though Randolf and the Tidings wouldn't see. "It's urgent."

"Hmm." The old man furrowed his brows and lips at once, tripling the already prominent wrinkles across his face such that his features blended one into the next in a most perplexing manner. "I suppose I can admit you to the front at least." He tittered to himself and turned back toward Natalya. "Just one fae—how much harm could you do?"

~

An impossibly boring half hour later, a steward of some kind deigned to allow Natalya inside, his sour expression and downturned mouth conveying his disapproval of her appearance and garb. She hadn't taken the sewers here, for shadows' sake. "Second stair-case on your left. One of the maids will show you." He spoke as though he'd willed his nasal passages closed from the inside and, with white-gloved hand, gestured that she might proceed deeper into the opulent house.

Natalya crept inside as gingerly as if she had arrived at the midnight hour on mission from the Tidings, though Randolf's attention had been far more focused on the docks than Nobles' Row of late. However lightly she stepped, the heels of her boots still clicked upon the marble floor. Most of the noble houses she'd entered had carpets that would muffle one's steps, oversized furni-ture to hide behind, and gaudy art dripping from the walls that cast helpful shadows to disappear within.

Atkinson's manse was without any of these material signs of wealth that, from what she gathered, served as a currency all its own among Serrana's courtiers, making the wide halls and ostentatiously papered rooms strangely cavernous in their emptiness.

Rounding the corner the steward had indicated, Natalya found a maid in a knee-length, dark blue dress waiting, her narrowed gaze observing Natalya's every breath as though she was personally responsible for the disappearance of the manse's finery.

"This way," the maid instructed. Her expression matched the distaste from the steward.

Not all of us stand about all day, Natalya thought, but there was no use defending herself from their judgements. She didn't envy the stasis of their way of life any more than they envied the active intrigue of hers.

The maid remained silent as she guided Natalya up the stairs. She gestured down another wide hallway toward an arched doorway with narrow double doors.

A similarly dressed serving girl waited outside what Natalya took to be Piper's chamber. Behind her, the first maid indicated that Natalya should be allowed to pass—as though either of them could have stopped her—and the second scurried to do as bidden.

"Miss, your visitor," the serving girl called softly, rapping twice against the door.

Natalya scanned the hallway, searching for hidden threats, marking the places where she would have obscured herself alongside the best exits if she needed to sneak Piper from the premises.

"Nata!" her sister squealed as the demure serving girl opened the double doors of her boudoir with averted gaze and a bowed head. Piper wore her long, dark hair tied back at the nape of her neck. A scarlet day gown accentuated her slender curves and offset the copper of her eyes. No limp to her step, no visible bruising—Piper was physically well.

Reassured that her sister was not in immediate danger, Natalya watched as the maid retreated back down the hallway. She was clad in linen and silk, a strange, round blue hat balanced atop her restrained curls.

So many strangers lurking around a half-dozen halls —no wonder her sister had been frightened.

Piper rushed to the door and launched herself at Natalya, capturing her around the waist and sending the pair of them careening back toward the gilded balcony that overlooked the main floor. "I'm so glad to see you," Piper sighed, meeting her sister's gaze with tears sparkling in her artfully shadowed eyes.

Natalya stiffly returned her sister's embrace, still unable to pinpoint the danger that had inspired Piper's panicked missive. "And I you," she murmured in Shadyn, the tongue of their ancestors that they'd grown up speaking with their mother in the forest. Natalya dropped her voice further so there would be no danger of being overheard. "Is it your maid who is threatening you?"

She could almost convince herself that the woman standing a carefully removed distance down the hall stiffened at Natalya's question, though there was little chance she'd overheard her words without magical aid. Natalya narrowed her gaze, watching the serving girl. It was exactly what she'd suspect of a noble, hiring a maid to spy on his courtesan, someone he supposedly cared for.

"Threatening me?" Piper answered in the common tongue and at a regular volume.

Natalya stepped back from her sister's embrace. It was clear Piper had been absent from La Consagrada for too long. She tapped her temple with long, fae eyebrow raised. "You asked for my help. Remember?"

"Oh." Piper smiled, suddenly recalling the urgent psychic missive she'd sent using Natalya's telepathy. "Yes, that." She gestured for Natalya to follow her into her opulent bedchamber. "Gretchen, I'll take tea in my rooms this morning. Please tell his lordship that my sister has arrived, and inform Edouard that I won't be taking any callers."

Piper caught Natalya's hand in hers, bouncing her way back into the room on her tiptoes.

"Yes, miss," the maid answered softly from the hall, shutting the doors behind Natalya and cutting off their surest route of escape.

Piper's shoulders fell the moment the doors latched into place. She squeezed Natalya's hand, avoiding her sister's gaze. Beneath her long lashes, her lips trembled.

It was the final sign of distress Natalya could stand. She tugged her hand out of Piper's grasp, immediately calling her blades into being. Sparkling, lilac daggers encrusted with glowing amethyst runes sprang to life in each of her palms. The house's security was so lax they hadn't even bothered to find the blades hidden within Natalya's boots. She likely could have gotten away with a dagger strapped to her outer thigh without the gate attendant even realizing.

"What is going on?" Natalya demanded, gaze shifting about the room. Several of her sister's trunks lay open, her few belongings resting in small stacks beside them, but nothing else was amiss.

Piper's breaths came unevenly, something that often happened as her distress increased.

"Did he hurt you?" Natalya spun the blade in her left hand and then her right. One for each of the nobleman's eyes, and then she'd work her way down. Slowly.

"No, Nata," Piper cried, catching her sister's wrists in her hands and attempting to drag them to rest at Natalya's sides.

Save Randolf and possibly Tomas, no one else would have dared seize Natalya with her blades out, not even in the ritualized blade dances she performed in the basement of La Consagrada. Natalya tightened her grip on the daggers, flipping them to point down and away from her sister's body.

"It's not Atkinson." Piper steadied herself, holding Natalya's gaze. "It's Randolf. I think."

Before the serving girl could return, Piper told Natalya of her Suzerain's financial troubles, the difficulty he kept encountering with finding buyers for the rare goods of his shipments. An entire cargo-hold had gone missing in Sanctuary just before Lord Atkinson had begun his courtship with Piper and invited her to move in with him. It had taken a month more before he owned up to any of the difficulties, and that was only after she'd started asking about the vanishing furniture.

A knock sounded against Piper's door, and Natalya whirled about on the cushioned chair, dagger at the ready.

"Easy," Piper soothed. She placed her hand over Natalya's fist, pressing the upraised dagger toward Natalya's lap.

Her sister rose, smoothing the fabric of her dress and rubbing her fingertips beneath her eyes to even out the lines of kohl. The dress swished as Piper crossed the room and opened the door.

Natalya kept her blades out of sight beneath the arms of the chair.

With an affected air of confidence, Piper plucked the tea tray from the servant's hands and carried it over to her sitting area, excusing Gretchen for the remainder of the morning. Over tea and sandwiches, she explained the various strategies Atkinson had pursued to become solvent again, each of which had failed more spectacularly than the last.

"He's finally found one among his peers whom he can confide in and who's willing to cover the taxes owed to the duke while he waits for his newest venture in the marshes to yield profits. But the rate of the borrowed taxes made me think of the Tidings."

Natalya frowned at the sandwich in her hand. The delicate, fluffy white bread was spread with a green paste and topped with a strangely crunchy slice of pale vegetable, its bitterness compounding the tea's unpleasant flavor. She cleared her throat, swallowing the mixture down.

"Why is that?" Her throat was dry from the odd sandwich. She'd tried her best to follow the ins and outs of Atkinson's fiscal woes, though she found it difficult to pity a man who employed so many to stand about while he, likewise, seemed to put forth very little effort at actually *doing* anything. Meanwhile, she and Tomas had been on ten raids in the past fortnight, squelching even the barest hint of the rumors that claimed the docks of Serrana were slipping out of the Tidings' control.

Piper shook her head. "You don't have to pretend to be unaware of his schemes in front of me. We're no longer children. I know what you had to do to survive."

Her sister's eyes were wide and sought to comfort her. And something else caught in her voice—pity.

Natalya tightened her jaw, her fingers beginning to twitch now that she'd put down the gooey sandwich. It was true she'd shielded Piper from Randolf's demands for a time, knowing her sister would object. She also understood that Ackley, the madam of La Consagrada who, alongside Randolf, had plucked the girls off the streets of Serrana, was making demands of Piper that Natalya would have objected to. But she wouldn't have spoken of such things with pity.

Even as girls in the forest, hidden away with their mother, Piper had dreamt of being a courtesan. Natalya had yet to find the romance Piper insisted was part and parcel of the courtiers' lives. It was all frippery and doldrums, never moving the world *toward* anything.

"*Perhaps it is best that we not speak such recollections aloud,*" Natalya thought to her sister, easily falling into the telepathic speech that she'd had since birth, one piece of the magical inheritance from their family line that, alongside her daggers, had fallen to her.

"They cannot understand us," Piper answered in Shadyn, her voice maintaining its stubbornly conversational volume.

"*I believe your maid understands our tongue,*" Natalya thought back.

She did not relish her sister's open laughter in reply and shot to her feet.

"No, Nata, wait, I'm sorry." Piper caught Natalya's hand. *"I know that Randolf has increased what he charges the nobles for docking, that he's lording his growing power over them, maybe even targeting my Suzerain on purpose."*

Natalya did not mistake the note of care in her sister's voice when mentioning the lord she'd contracted herself and her affections to. She eased her arm out of Piper's grasp, shaking her head. *"Why would he be targeting someone with nothing to give?"*

"Describing it as giving is generous."

Natalya glared back in answer. That was easy enough for Piper to say, removed from the hazards and deprivations of Serrana's streets. Half of what the Tidings took, they distributed to those in need. How many of the nobles could say the same?

"I have been on the raids of which you speak. Everyone pays the same rate. Yes, it's high, but it's not as though Duke Heinrik is exerting himself to protect the city from external threats. We keep them at bay."

Of all Randolf's policies, it was the one she believed in most fervently. If raiders, not to mention rival armies, knew that Serrana's docks were fiercely protected, they would be far less likely to attempt an attack by sea. And distributing the wealth and goods hoarded by the city's nobles was a welcome bonus alongside such steady employment.

Piper hadn't objected when she'd ferried secrets from high-brow visitors on the upper floor of La Consagrada, sending warnings to those like Natalya who worked beneath. What had the nobleman been trying to convince her of?

Her sister sighed, releasing her hand and sinking back amid the pile of her skirts onto the padded divan near the windows of her chamber. The elegant silks suited Piper—the deep red bringing out the sensuousness of her frame and drama of her features. They were no longer gar in the woods.

Natalya didn't envy Piper her position—she'd happily keep her ink-dyed wool and leathers.

"I was afraid you'd say that." Piper stared absently out the towering row of windows. "We're downsizing, relocating to a smaller estate while Atkinson's friend helps him get everything back in order."

"Do you know the name of this friend?" Natalya asked, wanting to offer her sister something, even if she couldn't provide the comfort that her Suzerain was being robbed of his wealth at dagger-point rather than through his own incompetence.

"No," Piper whispered, slumping further back into her seat.

Natalya turned about, at a loss for what to do within courtiers' society.

"Perhaps you can help me pack?" Piper suggested, brightening slightly. "You're far better company than the maids."

She assented and spent the next two hours assisting Piper with an impossible number of small silk and lace garments they had to carefully fold and arrange within Piper's trunks. More undergarments than implements of self-protection.

Her sister's mood lifted as they worked, and she told Natalya of her various social engagements, the friends she'd made among the courtier class.

Natalya offered what polite conversation she could while unease for her sister knotted her stomach. Piper and their mother had foreseen a future with both girls as courtesans, a future that, Piper promised, was an especially happy one for Natalya. But the reality of the courtiers' existence fell short of the elegance and ease her sister had dreamt of, though she refused to say as much aloud.

It reminded her of helping Piper pack a single trunk when she was leaving La Consagrada only a few weeks before and moving in with the Suzerain who swore he couldn't live without her. Regardless of her own fears, Natalya wouldn't be the one to steal the glee from her sister's expression. A glee that had quickly faded to the same fierce determination Natalya knew well.

Instead, she repeated to Piper what she'd said when her sister brought her the news about Atkinson's suit. "He's lucky to have you by his side." She'd smirked a little, thinking of the Suzerain who had been overtaken by her sister like a crashing wave. "Someone who knows how to fight for those she cares for."

Piper had hugged her around the waist then. "I've always had that," she said with a smile.

This time her smile was sad. "I can only hope so."

CHAPTER 2
NATALYA

THREE WEEKS LATER

Natalya and Tomas crouched outside the Oxbrow manor, staring up at the cold stone edifice. Natalya didn't have her mother and sister's gift for prophecy, but the estate made the hair along the back of her neck prickle all the same. 'Lower your hackles,' Piper would have told her if she were here.

But that was just it. Piper had disappeared inside three days ago, her psychic connection to Natalya immediately severed. Natalya hadn't felt her sister since.

Tomas was the only one willing to go against Randolf's orders to scope out the estate with Natalya. He shifted nervously beside her. "We'll need to be getting back soon."

"Randolf's price-gouging at the docks can wait," she answered without turning toward her friend. "Piper needs us."

He flinched, not wanting to argue with her and not

wanting to defy the Tidings' leader. Any degree of concern on Piper's behalf was a sharp contrast to how Randolf had reacted when Natalya brought him her devastating news about the duel and sudden death of Piper's Suzerain a few days before and how, by Draykemire's law, her sister's courtesan contract passed to the nobleman who had slain her lover.

"Worry not about your sister, little blade," Randolf had answered with a quick wave of his hand. "As cushy as the life of a courtesan is compared to ours, there are still obstacles Piper must navigate." He shook his head, regarding her, sensing that Natalya wasn't satisfied with his placating. "She has trained for this in her years working upstairs. Your sister is exactly where I want her to be."

Natalya had tightened her hands into fists, suppressing her blades. No need to confess to Randolf the depths of her concern for Piper or the extent to which this conversation was agitating her.

His gaze had narrowed, studying Natalya, a dangerous shift in his demeanor that would have reduced even the most confident merchants and thieves of Serrana's docks into a puddle of sweat. But not Natalya. Randolf needed her. And she needed her sister to be safe.

"Are we going to be at odds, little blade?" A chill swept over his voice, sharpening its steel. "Or are you going to put to work the skills that earned you your place within my ranks all those years ago?" His cold blue eyes glinted with the unstated threat. With the merest whim, he could return her to the streets to fend for herself, this time with no Piper to ground and guide her and with every thief and smuggler in the city set against her.

Natalya swallowed the fear for her sister. Another port raid, the next in a carefully planned series targeting multiple ships within the fortnight ranked more highly with Randolf than her concerns for her sister's well-being. "I'll keep my place."

Randolf had beamed. "Good!" He threw his arms out to the side in the magnanimous gesture he used to charm merchants and dim-witted guards. "Take Tomas with you tonight. The lads will be waiting when the two of you are through."

The great stone house that had swallowed Piper and severed her telepathic connection to her sister would also be waiting for her when she'd helped Randolf extract his penance from the merchants docking in Serrana who had the audacity to try to avoid the duke's rates *and* Randolf's private toll. "They need to be reminded of who holds the true power here, little blade," he said before dismissing her from his study. "Not the nobles. Not the priestesses. Certainly not the duke." He'd grinned widely, a flash of white that didn't change his eyes. "Me."

Natalya nodded, accepting his reminder. She smiled to herself after she slipped out of Randolf's study. She'd been planning to bring Tomas along with her anyway— and with several hours till sunset, they had time to return to Oxbrow's manor to search for signs of Piper before doubling back to the docks.

It was the first she'd spoken to Randolf in weeks. After her visit with Piper, the rapport they'd known for years had unraveled in a matter of hours. The city watch tightened its hold on the docks, rounding up the Tidings with an efficiency that could only be attributed to insider knowledge of their plans. Natalya had gone from favored blade to first suspect with her open questioning of Randolf's methods and the suspicion she could be conspiring with a courtesan and her Suzerain. Randolf had locked her away within La Consagrada while he determined her loyalty. She saw neither sun nor moonlight for three days.

Eventually, Randolf had relented, though even now, his accusations twinged at the base of her neck. She could prove herself tonight, then Randolf and the others would see.

Tomas quickly acquiesced to Natalya's plan—a quick check on Piper, she'd promised, and then to the docks.

Back on Nobles' Row, her stomach twisted. Could she simply depart from the manor imprisoning Piper now that she was here? Natalya shifted her weight onto her heels and leaned her back against the stone wall that surrounded the Oxbrow manor's grounds. Despite Randolf's punishment, she'd been right to rush to her sister's aid, even if nothing had come of it.

Unlike Atkinson's first estate or the more modest quarters where he'd relocated his household—further debasing his rank to settle within the merchants' quarter —Oxbrow's manse was palatial in size, squatting upon a double lot in the center of Nobles' Row, an upgrade in status only a couple of years old, from what she understood. Only the duke's residence was more grand.

Peering around the stone column through an iron

gate meant as a side entrance for night patrols and gardeners, Natalya weighed the concerns she had for her sister with the threats hidden beneath Randolf's warnings. "One chance, little blade. One misstep, and you're back beneath."

Tomas eyed her nervously. Of the two of them, he was the better informed of Randolf's plans now, outranking Natalya in the Tidings for the first time in their many years of friendship. "We need to go," Tomas urged, their mission at the docks beginning to make him antsy.

Natalya searched the stone edifice, reading into every shadow, every closed curtain, desperate to find some sign of her sister. Was Piper alive? Natalya clenched her jaw. She would know if it had come to that—would sense it, and Serrana, however corrupt, was not so lawless as to leave one of its prize courtesans without the fanfare of mourning. The thought made her senses swim.

She stepped up to the gate itself, ignoring Tomas's hiss of caution, and wrapped her hands around the iron bars. Despite the warmth of the spring sunshine, they were rough and cold in her grasp. The gate was higher than Atkinson's had been, but not so high as to be able to keep her from her sister for much longer.

"You there," a guard called from inside, his gait an easy march, gaze narrowed. "There's not cause for you to be loitering about." He made a shooing motion with his hand, revealing a shining hilt tucked into his scabbard.

Natalya suppressed a smirk at the polished steel. What was the likelihood he'd used it in the past fortnight, whereas she'd felled three unruly sailors only the evening before. They'd tried to run when Randolf initiated his search of their cargo, believing they could escape when he found they'd tried to cheat him of half the percentage due on their wares by only handing over a partial shipping manifest.

"Do you control the street now?" Tomas shot back before Natalya could respond to the guard's instructions.

The man's eyes narrowed further. Unlike Natalya, Tomas had to wear his blades openly on his person. "I do when riff-raff decides to muddy up the border of my lord's property," he huffed.

Tomas grunted in delight as the guard strode forward and grimaced, his face scrunching as he paled, throat bobbing.

He'd gotten near enough to smell the sewers on them —muddied up indeed. With Randolf's deadline for taking their posts for tonight's raid fast approaching, she hadn't had time for the clogged traffic of high street within the merchants' quarter. They'd taken the most direct route here, through filth and sludge.

"Come on," Natalya urged, tugging at Tomas's sleeve. The guard would recover himself soon enough, and he'd call for reinforcements.

Tomas jerked away from her, puffing out his thin chest at the guard's insult to street urchins like himself and Natalya. "I'll have you know—"

"Not *now*," Natalya insisted, grabbing him by the arm and dragging him off.

Behind them, the guard doubled over, gagging, while waving for help.

"Do you think we really smell *that* bad?" Tomas

whispered as they rounded a verdant corner and disappeared behind a different noble's ostentatious display of shrubbery.

Tomas's question and the hopelessness of her quest to aid Piper hit her all at once. Natalya snorted a laugh, finding little other possible reaction to her current situation. "Yes, I believe so," she answered, cheering ever so slightly at Tomas's grin. "Though he seemed especially sensitive for a perimeter guard."

She nodded in the direction of the docks, where the next phase of their current mission for Randolf awaited. They'd stomp through one of the public creeks on the way rather than taking the sewers. She wanted those paths to be clear for when she snuck back that night. It might be easier for Piper to get a signal to her with the aid of the darkness. And signal or no, she wasn't waiting any longer.

CHAPTER 3
PIPER

Piper pressed her lips together as she scrubbed her hands above the porcelain basin left within her rooms. The remembered scent of blood still clung to her swollen nostrils. So much blood.

Her new Suzerain, Lord Felix Oxbrow, had challenged her true Suzerain, Lord Horatio Atkinson, based on a debt owed from his shipping taxes, borrowed at a usurious rate from the Oxbrow house in the guise of offering aid. Through the months of their courtship, she'd watched Lord Atkinson's concern for his estate grow with each passing week as cargo was confiscated at the docks, both those bordering Serrana from the sea and the river passing the supplies to the rest of Draykemire.

He'd promised to speak to the duke about his situation and the growing instability of trade in the region. Someone needed to intervene, he said, ideally the duke before nobles like himself had to take matters into their own hands.

Piper's thoughts had immediately gone to her sister, to Natalya's insistence that the ruin of Lord Atkinson's estate had nothing to do with special targeting on behalf of Randolf. She couldn't inform her Suzerain of her conversation with her sister without risking Natalya being locked away within Serrana's prisons or made a target of the nobles' ire, a far worse fate than she'd find at the city's hands. Piper had even gone so far as to lie to Lord Atkinson about who her visitor was, "a fellow fae friend she'd met at La Consagrada."

She didn't realize her fears were pointed in the wrong direction until it was too late.

The day before his meeting with Duke Heinrik, Oxbrow had appeared at their door in the merchants' district, demanding immediate recompense for the debts owed to his house. "Face me, now, or depart from the city in disgrace, leaving your few remaining belongings behind," Oxbrow had demanded, a crazed gleam in his eye.

Piper only heard about Oxbrow's impossible demand after the fact. He had to have known that to Atkinson, the options he pretended to offer were one and the same.

Had she known what was coming, she never would have been present for the combat. Atkinson was portly, older, somewhat slow, but he'd been exceedingly kind to her. His intelligence and sense of humor had wooed her from the upper floors of La Consagrada into days and then weeks in his private residence. When he made her his offer, she'd been equal parts surprised and flattered, and she couldn't find it in herself to refuse.

His confrontation with Oxbrow had unfurled quickly, out in the open in the front room of their house. Edouard, head of the serving staff, had rushed into the breakfast parlor where Piper was preparing the tea for herself and Atkinson, a tradition she'd grown fond of and only broke in extreme circumstances, such as Natalya's visit.

Hearing the raised voices coming from just beyond the parlor door, Piper had lowered the delicately flowered kettle and started toward the sound. Edouard stopped her, wrapping an arm around her waist and tugging her to the side of the room, a finger pressed upon her lips.

Had he performed the same protective act for her sister and not herself, he would have gotten a magically summoned blade plunged into his gut for his troubles. But Piper had studied different tricks, different modes of protection in La Consagrada's upper floors than those that had served Natalya in the dimly lit basement parlor.

While Lords Atkinson and Oxbrow yelled at one another, Piper's thoughts flickered over to her second futile attempt at protecting her Suzerain from his fate a few days before. After their move to the merchants' district, she'd returned to the only place she knew to ask for relief from the crushing weight of Atkinson's debt to the nobleman offering him counsel on how to slide out from beneath it.

Her trip to see Randolf required another lie to her Suzerain, saying that she was going to purchase memory candles in honor of her mother. She'd paid the carriage driver for his discretion and had him take her to La Consagrada instead.

Just as Piper had predicted he would, Randolf had forced her to wait. Whether he was trying to prevent Natalya from knowing she was present or simply asserting his view of where she stood within the hierarchy of the Tidings, she wasn't sure. Piper didn't mind the secrecy from Natalya. She had already involved her sister once and, until matters settled, would not do so again.

Finally, Randolf deigned to meet with her in the corner booth of the smoky underground gambling den. "Well, get to it," Randolf spat by way of greeting.

Piper knotted her fingers in her lap but forced herself to straighten, meeting the stone of Randolf's pale blue gaze. "I've come to ask for your help. My Suzerain is in trouble."

"Ha! And here I thought you were too good for the likes of me," Randolf had sneered, his upper lip curling as his gaze slowly swept over her recently purchased finery. Lord Atkinson had refused her request that he temporarily reduce spending for her attire.

Piper remained still under Randolf's scrutiny, refusing to allow the shame he wanted her to feel to color her cheeks. The leader of the Tidings had never reacted to her or the girls upstairs the way most men and many women, regardless of class, did. It was that lack, rather than the initial observation, that had allowed her to notice what *did* darken Randolf's gaze and tighten his jaw.

On one of the few missions she'd undertaken with Natalya for him, Randolf had accompanied them as well.

The possessive, predatory way he'd watch the blades appear in her sister's hands, his soft grunt of satisfaction when she plunged them into the first mate's neck for resisting Randolf's extortion—when he looked at Piper and other courtesans, he saw only common whores, but with Natalya, he saw something exquisite.

Piper didn't fault him for that. If the risk weren't so great, she might have brought Natalya with her to make her case, but Randolf was paranoid of betrayal, likely especially where Natalya was concerned, knowing that she was a weak spot in his otherwise impenetrable hide. Atkinson's fortune wasn't worth the harm that would befall her sister during the interrogation Randolf's suspicions would demand.

Midway through her plea, he'd refused to help her Suzerain. "There will be little enough room for parasites like yours in the world to come," Randolf had warned. "You chose your side. Begone."

Shortly thereafter, Atkinson experienced his greatest loss to date, and Piper had no doubt of who was to blame.

She didn't dare confess her suspicions to her grieving lord, who could no longer keep secret the sale of his household possessions, each piece carefully acquired through generations and lost in a matter of days. He refused to touch the dowry set aside for Piper should she wish to end their courtship and take up with another Suzerain instead.

Through those brief, difficult days between her visit

to Randolf and Oxbrow's coming to collect his dues, the leader of the Tidings held two axes over Piper's head that secured her silence—her sister's safety and a hole-ridden net to catch Piper from the jaws of defeat if her Suzerain should be fully knocked from his position in society.

Atkinson had been run through with a dueling sword instead. Edouard could hold her back no longer at Atkinson's cry of pain. Oxbrow's footsteps were already fading deeper into the house.

Piper had sprinted into the front room, screaming for the guards and kneeling at her Suzerain's side.

With tears gleaming in his eyes, it had been Edouard who laid out Oxbrow's terms for Piper's future less than an hour later—return to La Consagrada, surrendering the place in society she'd fought so hard for, having ascended from refugee in the wilderness to high-society whore to courtesan—or keep her place as a courtesan and transfer her loyalty and services to the man who'd won his rival's estate through deeper pockets and the end of a blade.

Piper's lip had trembled only slightly, the decision made long before, in childhood in the forest where she dreamt of her future in the city, the finery she'd experience on the arm of a doting lord paling in comparison to the dazzling future she knew awaited her sister along a similar path. "I'll stay," she whispered.

Mamaun had shared the same visions. It was the girls' destiny to become courtesans, and they were halfway there.

Edouard had dropped his head, the tears falling without words.

He scratched her name onto the ledger of the estate's goods that would transfer, sealing her fate. Three days had passed since then.

"Cleansing ourselves again, are we?" Oxbrow leaned against the archway of Piper's bathing chamber, that same curl of judgement contorting the shallow line of his lips as Randolf had worn the day she asked for his help with her lord's financial affairs. Seeing the affluence and lack of distress—indeed, the utter confidence of Oxbrow's purse—she had little doubt of the connection between the nobleman and the Tidings' leader. She simply needed a way to prove it.

"It's chief among the courtesan values, is it not?"

Oxbrow huffed, kicking himself off the door and pacing within the tiled chamber instead, rounding nearer to Piper with each pass. His boots clicked upon the floor, marking the impatience of his movements, each rap of his metal-tipped soles causing the muscles along her spine and shoulders to seize. "That depends upon whom one asks, I'm sure. Something they would have taught you in the first weeks of a courtesan academy had you possessed the breeding and funds to attend such an institution."

Piper patted the water from her hands with the towel kept beside the basin, never fully turning her back on her new Suzerain or removing him from her gaze. Lord Atkinson hadn't minded that she hadn't been trained as so many of the others had. Her chest tightened as she realized, too late, that the reason for that might have been his own financial woes rather than any degree to which he was smitten with her, as she'd thought at the time.

Lord Oxbrow slowed in his pacing and spun about, facing Piper and blocking her exit from the room. "My guards have made a most interesting report of a young fae woman and a gangly urchin squatting outside my gates, trying to peer inside."

Piper's heart shuddered against the confines of her chest, doubling the rate of her pulse. She cursed herself for the sudden intake of breath, her inability to move.

"The fae they described sounds nothing like you—more fighter or thief than aspiring courtier. The more eloquent among them described her as 'moonstone and amethyst' to your onyx and garnet." Oxbrow's lips twisted into a foul, sideways smile. "I must admit, I was intrigued."

He gestured out of the room, lingering in the doorway so that she would have to squeeze past him, her skirts bunching between the nobleman and the door before she could escape to the other side.

The moment she did, Oxbrow seized her elbow, his grip vice-like in its insistence.

Piper imagined roots springing from her heels, anchoring her in place, protecting her like the great oaks of the forest where she and Natalya had grown up. Her magic didn't work that way. Since she wasn't an earthshaper or a druid, no such protections appeared.

"Does that sound like anyone you know?" His breath was a hot cloud, growling and wet against her ear, the stubble of his goatee scratching against her skin. The sour scent of alcohol on his breath made her want to retch.

"A scrawny boy? No."

"Bah!"

Piper jolted away from his bark of laughter, spittle striking her ear and lodging in her hair.

"I underestimated how humorous you are," Oxbrow observed as though congratulating himself on a personal cleverness. He tugged her arm into his side and grasped it with his opposite hand, holding her fast as he guided her out of her private bedchamber down the hall toward the rooms he shared with his twin courtesans. "The lad is a known associate of the Tidings and their leader, Randolf. A dreadful man, to be sure, but a powerful one."

Midway down the hall, two of Oxbrow's household guard fell into step behind the nobleman and Piper, lingering near enough to grab her by the hair if she decided to run.

Piper searched the hall around her, chest tightening with each step. The rounded end of the hallway widened as a tunnel before her eyes.

"The 'uncommonly pretty' fae, as one of the guards put it, has a great deal in common with a certain terror of the city's docks if you could believe it. One they call 'the Blade,' said to be so subtle and so violent that by the time one of her victims senses her presence, she's already slit their throat."

A narrow doorway she'd never before noticed hung open beside the door to Oxbrow's chamber. Two more guards waited outside it, another pair by the arched windows.

"After talking matters over with my head of security, he fears that some recent unpleasantness at the docks may have upset the Tidings—a misunderstanding, as it were." Oxbrow wore his face as a mask, but an unhinged rage rippled off of his taut form. "For your own protection, you're being moved until we discover who these snooping figures are and what they want. And," he chuckled to himself, "until Randolf has the wisdom to set aside his pride and accept the, hmm, changing tides, shall we say?"

In a smoother motion than she would have thought possible, Oxbrow shoved Piper into the round, stone chamber. One of the guards slammed the door shut behind her.

Piper cringed as the echo died down, taking stock of her new environment.

Against one wall was a bedroll and blanket. Against the other was a tall table with a wood and leather chest like an apothecary might carry resting atop it, an array of needles and vials laid out on a cloth beside the chest.

Something deep in Piper's stomach clenched at the sight and bade her to keep as far from the chest as she could. She wandered over to the opposite side of the room, tucked the blanket around her shoulders, and sank onto the floor.

"What have I done?" she whispered, the last several days returning to her in disordered flashes. Natalya's certainty, Randolf's confident disdain, Edouard's grief.

Oxbrow's words spun around and around her mind. Did he mean to harm the Tidings? Had he already? She clutched the blanket and leaned into the stone.

"Nata?" she thought, her sister's voice strangely absent from her mind.

When was the last time she'd heard from Natalya? So much had happened in the aftermath of her Suzerain's death. She'd told Natalya what she could of what had transpired, but after?

Piper lowered her head onto her raised knees and shut her eyes. *"Nata!"*

CHAPTER 4
RANDOLF

Randolf sat back from the scratched wooden desk tucked away within his office in the basement of La Consagrada. The leather of his chair was smooth and soft beneath his grip—precisely the way he imagined the neck of whichever nobleman was responsible for these cursed counter-raids against the Tidings would feel beneath his grasp.

A dozen raids in as many nights. Ruined. Trained bandits, so skilled as to have been working for him for years without incident, rounded up, their movements anticipated by the most bumbling of the city watch.

At enormous expense, he'd bailed them out. Despite his careful stockpiles of gold and provisions, at this rate the Tidings would be defunct within months. His life's work, destroyed.

A familiar knock sounded against his door.

Randolf sighed, forcing the tension from his shoulders. He refused to let his crew see how dire their situation had grown. If they knew how tenuous his hold upon the veins of commerce in and out of Serrana suddenly was, they'd bolt. The few who stayed would never trust him again. "Come in."

"Begging your pardon, sir—"

Tomas, yet again, with more carefully rehearsed arguments for why Randolf should renew his trust in Natalya after her release from the Tidings' prison. At least his over-eager precautions had kept her safe from the city watch.

"What is it, lad?"

"A nobleman, sir, and"—Tomas swallowed thickly—"an entire regiment of the duke's guard."

Randolf nodded slowly. Whoever it was who'd been out-gaming the Tidings was here to up their ante, propose terms. "Send him in."

The sneering, ornately clad form of Lord Felix Oxbrow slid into view, casting his disproportionate shadow across Randolf's doorway.

Oxbrow. He ought to have known.

"Quite a stir you've caused of late." Randolf scowled at the nobleman, the one who'd driven yet another rift between himself and Natalya, bringing her fear for her sister to impossible heights and riling his temper in turn.

How many times had Ackley mentioned taking Natalya off his hands and sending her to work upstairs? How much coin had he turned down, the disgusting bribes of nobles like this one offering to pay a fortnight's worth of raids for a few nights with Natalya? Like she'd take them, he'd groused to Ackley more than once. The madam only raised her eyebrow in answer, urging him to doubt his instincts where the fae was concerned, but she knew better than to bring the offers to Natalya herself.

Randolf was certain it was only a matter of time before he gained Natalya's regard. Before this business with the disrupted raids and then Piper's deceased Suzerain, he'd believed he was well on his way to achieving that objective. He fixed Oxbrow in his sights— he was the one orchestrating the events that had eroded Randolf's progress in winning Natalya over. Her accusations, not to mention their timing, had left him with little choice. Three days in lock-up, for questionable loyalty. But it hadn't been Natalya conspiring with Atkinson to shift the Tidings out from beneath Randolf's feet. He should have recognized Oxbrow's manipulative hand far sooner, before he set ablaze everything he'd built with her.

"Is there trouble in your house as well as mine?" Oxbrow smiled, bemused at the Tidings' plight.

Randolf struggled not to roll his eyes. "The only trouble in your house is that of your own making. Why kill Atkinson rather than slowly bleed him dry?"

The nobleman's grin widened. "Worked out my place in all that, did you?"

He bobbed his chin, a minimal acknowledgement. "Rob a man to ruin, and he can no longer swell your coffers." Randolf shook his head. "Not my style." He hadn't noticed anything amiss with the shipping patterns, coming or outgoing, until Piper relocated from the upstairs to Atkinson's house. It was simple concern, really, as much for Piper's interests as the ways in which they might splash over to Natalya that had him digging into the man's finances and smelling rot.

"Perhaps you take too small a view of the field of play." Oxbrow sauntered deeper into Randolf's office, his nobleman's false confidence deluding him into believing he was welcome everywhere when it couldn't have been further from the truth.

Oxbrow's upper lip curled as he glanced about the office, no doubt dismayed by its size. Randolf wouldn't expect someone like Oxbrow to know the discipline required to be measured in all things, to recognize when intimidation was beneficial and when it was not. Most of the Tidings had grown up in homes the size of this room. It carried all the status it needed to without unnecessary pomp that would make his crew doubt him.

"For a man who cares for little beyond his own affairs, that's a strange accusation to make," Randolf answered.

Oxbrow plopped himself down onto the chair opposite Randolf's, reclining immediately and tucking his hands behind his head, elbows spread wide. "Oh ho, touched on a nerve, have I?" The nobleman's glinting grin returned. It did no favors to the narrow angles of his visage. "You know that the duke has recently appointed me as his chief adviser." His smile twisted wider, and he angled his gaze to stare directly at Randolf. "Would you believe that it was my promise to help His Grace rein in the bandit problem frightening away commerce from Serrana's shores that was the final feather in the cap of my suit for a promotion?"

Randolf tightened his jaw. He'd been right to suspect

a rat, though he shouldn't have suspected Natalya so quickly. The thought of her with nobleman scum like this one—

"Of course I'm happy to go back to the way things were," Oxbrow offered, head tilted to the side.

"You'd turn on the duke so easily? Why?"

The nobleman shrugged. "Let's just say that there's plenty Heinrik misses and will continue to be unaware of." He waved his hand as though swatting away a fly, so little regard did he bear toward the sovereign.

Randolf couldn't fault Oxbrow for that. Without the queen's backing and the support of the Gaian priestesses in maintaining the goodwill of the region, Heinrik would have lost the Serra Valley within weeks of his coronation. He crossed his arms over his chest. "I prefer straightforward terms in business matters. Speak plainly."

"As you wish." Oxbrow unfolded himself like a gangly sailor's knot, leaning nearer to Randolf in an unwise gesture of unreciprocated intimacy. "As you know, I have recently acquired a valuable asset by way of one Miss Piper Slipshayde, upstart courtesan and former employee and spy of yourself and Madam Ackley." Oxbrow raised an eyebrow.

"Imagine my delight in discovering that this Miss Slipshayde is the sole living relative of one Miss Natalya Slipshayde, known simply as the Blade in merchants' circles, the feared shard of moonlight in the night." That sickening, twisted grin returned. "My terms are thus— Piper is to remain under my control *and* under my protection. Under no circumstances are you to interfere."

Randolf's eyes narrowed further. Given Natalya's

panic at the change in her sister's living accommodations, he'd already made a few discreet inquiries as to her safety and the legalities involved in her relocation.

The man across from him was playing several steps ahead and, from the look of him, planning something untoward where Piper was concerned. "She agreed to her courtesan's contract passing over to you rather than lowering her social position to return here." Whatever game Oxbrow was playing, he wouldn't be outmaneuvered. "Why are you assuming I would defy her expressed wishes?"

Oxbrow's eyes gleamed with the same self-satisfaction of a feral cat cornering a sea rat, and Randolf realized, too late, his series of mistakes in the girls' affairs. "Because I have in my possession what Natalya wants more than anything in the world." Oxbrow dropped his voice from its sharp, nasal tones, showing for the first time since his arrival the back-stabbing mastermind behind the usurping of the duke's right hand, making him for all intents and purposes the functional ruler of the Serra Valley. "And seeing how Natalya is that same weakness for *you*, I think you'll understand what a repositioning that means for the two of us as far as our negotiations are concerned."

He tried to deny the cold prickles of sweat against the base of his spine, the twinge at the base of his neck. "I won't hand her over to you."

"No." Oxbrow beamed. "What you will do is this—allow her to fall into my trap or lose every scrap, every barrel, every coin you've ever taken. Stay out of my way, or I will order the guards to execute the Tidings on sight.

And just like that"—Oxbrow snapped his fingers—"I exterminate the very memory of the Tidings from the city, and Natalya finds herself truly alone in the world."

The nobleman smirked at Randolf, confident in his outmaneuvering of the Tidings' leader. "Imagine who she will turn to then."

It was the utter confidence of Oxbrow's terms that shook Randolf. To make such a threat with no way of backing it . . . "Who's in your pocket that you'd come here and present me with such a threat?" This wasn't the first time a noble had tried to buy him, and Randolf hoped it wouldn't be the last.

Oxbrow was the first to attempt such a personal form of negotiation, curse them both.

"Let's just say it's someone with the power to bring the whole of Serrana down upon your ears and, should they wish, bring the kingdom to its knees shortly thereafter." Oxbrow wiped at the corners of his lips. "Someone you're in no position to cross."

The presence of the duke's soldiers within La Consagrada wasn't the sole cause of the swelling of Oxbrow's confidence. The nobleman was the mouthpiece, but someone else was tugging upon the strings. He had to find out who the puppeteer was and quickly.

The situation within Serrana had deteriorated even faster than Randolf had believed an hour before. A rat in his midst had sold out the entirety of his organization to this snake, and here the snake was, threatening Natalya. Randolf swallowed his rising dread and attempted to reassert the cold, languid ease he was known for. "Sate my curiosity then—" He resisted the urge to clear his throat as though he could dislodge the quaver that had already escaped upon his voice. "Natalya and Piper, fae from the forest, refugees turned orphans turned bandit and courtesan. What could so powerful a figure want with them?"

The answering glint confirmed Randolf's worst suspicions. "If all goes right—and it will—they're more valuable than you could possibly imagine."

Their time was growing short and Randolf's already thin patience was beginning to fray. He needed to shore up his position within Serrana *now*. There was a fault in Oxbrow's terms—one he had helped to put into place. Natalya distrusted nobles. That was part of why he'd been so quickly thrown by her coming to Atkinson's defense. Moments into Natalya's plea, Randolf had convinced himself that Atkinson had made a suit Natalya intended to take, swindling Randolf on her way out, possibly taking the loyalty of the Tidings with her.

Oxbrow's manipulation was far wider reaching than anything he'd suspected on his own. Randolf ground his teeth. The nobleman had been right that he'd taken too narrow a view, but it wasn't a mistake he'd make again.

"Natalya won't walk into your trap simply because you set it." He'd think of something better, something that wasn't half-bluster, when he had more time, after he got this foul man out of his office and found a way to get Natalya out of the city, some excuse or promise of grandeur—something strong enough to pull her away from her sister until Randolf was able to rescue Piper from Oxbrow's hold.

"That may be," Oxbrow sneered, "but she cares too

much for Piper to just leave her sister trapped. I think you and I both know how weak that makes her in this particular circumstance."

The nobleman didn't have to say the other half of his insinuation aloud—as weak as *you* made yourself in this exchange.

Oxbrow rose from his seat. "I'll send the lad in, shall I?" His grin widened. "Do give dear Natalya my best." With two paces left between himself and the door, Oxbrow hesitated. "Oh, and if you opt to warn Natalya, I'll have her killed in front of you." His sideways grin flashed before he turned back toward the door. "I'll be watching." He waggled his fingers in a farewell wave.

When the door finally slammed shut behind him, Randolf collapsed backward into the worn padding of his chair. Everything he'd worked for, all he'd built—it was all destroyed. Wormed away from under his grasp by a nobleman. Natalya had tried to warn him, and he'd punished her instead. And now? He'd failed to protect his own, and Natalya and Piper would be the ones to pay.

The choice Oxbrow had placed before Randolf was clear. Natalya or the Tidings.

His stomach churned. It was an easy choice to make. Easier than it should have been. He could only hope that, when the time came, he was capable of seeing it through.

CHAPTER 5
NATALYA

Natalya and Tomas carved their way through the city, washing the stench of the sewers from their boots as best they could before taking their positions as Randolf had ordered, hidden just before sunset, ready to take out the skeleton crew left aboard while the rest took their shore leave.

Unlike their usual arrangement, following her demotion, Natalya's orders were coming through Tomas rather than Randolf giving them to her. "You're sure this is the correct ship?" Natalya nodded toward the docked vessel, blocked in by the city's levy system.

Randolf paid the dockmistress handsomely and always knew which ships to strike.

"Yes, I promise," Tomas reassured her. "We just need to hold tight and wait for the signal."

It came as night settled around the docks. A shrill bird's call, caught upon the breeze. The Tidings had adopted the song of the Shadowlands nightingale as their own. Easy to pick out as the birds wisely avoided the city, sticking to the forests where hidden portals might release them back to their homeland.

Natalya slunk out of her hiding place, checking the set of her hood over her moon-white hair. Being slighter and swifter than most of the Tidings also meant she was usually the first on board when they were conducting a raid, the first into the tunnels when they were orchestrating a robbery.

She knew without needing to check that Tomas would be right behind her, at least until they boarded the ship. It was his job to secure anyone hiding below, hers to ensure the top deck was clear before the others climbed aboard to subdue any stragglers and begin removing cargo.

As a shadow passed over the greater moon, Natalya crouched low and stole up the gangplank. There was a creaking lantern at the sterncastle, and two others carried by sailors on night watch.

The lantern-bearers paced the decks, one slower than the other. She'd target the laggard first.

Natalya tried not to think about the sailors on jobs like this one. Tonight, the stakes for her were too high. Failing here would prevent her from rescuing Piper, a price she wasn't willing to pay, whatever misgivings about the Tidings she'd had over the last few weeks.

Piper's world hadn't been the only one to crash in around her.

The creaks in the rigging overhead and the lapping of the levy against the side of the ship drowned out the whisper of Natalya's footsteps as she snuck toward the first watchman. He walked with a stoop and a slight limp.

She timed her steps to his and willed one of her blades into her hand. The familiar lilac glow of her dagger soothed her. She dropped into the rhythm of what she had to do. Steady breath in, steady out—Natalya lunged, jabbing her blade into the sailor's gut once, twice, thrice.

The man groaned, doubling over in pain and shock. A death gasp rattled in his throat as he searched her hooded face to meet her gaze. His widened in recognition—her amethyst eyes had a reputation all their own—and he collapsed onto the deck.

"Arnold?" the other watchman called.

Natalya stole into the darkness beside one of the large wooden crates the sailors had brought onto the deck for unloading. Had they complied with Randolf's demands, they would have left his payment upon the dock.

She left the blade in the first sailor's chest, allowing its glow to deepen the shadows behind the crate.

"You fallen again?"

Steady in, steady out.

The second watcher stomped across the deck, her heavy leather coat disguising her slighter frame.

Natalya shut her eyes. *It's just another sailor. She's no different than any of the others. It doesn't matter that she might have a sister waiting for her to return home.*

She stilled the shaking in her hands, a side-effect of the time she'd spent locked within the bowels of La

Consagrada's basement after her confrontation with Randolf three weeks before.

Piper needed her to be present. Now.

"By Gaia, Arnold—"

A blade in each hand, Natalya sprang out of the shadows and launched herself toward the sailor. She feinted to one side, sending the woman tripping backward, nearly losing her balance, exposing her leg beneath the flaps of her leather coat.

Natalya slashed a blade across the inside of the woman's thigh.

The sailor screamed, waving her lantern before her as she tried to smash it against Natalya's head.

She ducked beneath it, rolling over the dead man's body and plucking the blade from his chest. She flicked one of her daggers toward the woman who'd finally drawn the scimitar from her belt and blocked Natalya's blade with her own.

Natalya's answering grin echoed the crescent of the lesser moon overhead. Finally an interesting opponent.

The sailor backed toward the center of the deck, her stance wide and low to preserve her balance. Without watching Natalya's feet, she matched her, step for step. A trained protector, perhaps, or one brought on to help with security aboard the ship. Had she received the orders from Randolf, Natalya would have known the manifest details, how much protection to expect, how much of a fight.

"He had three children," the woman spat at Natalya. "He deserved better than to be cut down by scum like you—"

Natalya tossed her second blade lower than she had the first, aiming for the hollow above the woman's hip. It pierced through the soft fabrics beneath the leather with a whisper, and the woman cried out in pain.

In trying to block the thrown blade, the woman had turned to the side, collapsing over the vulnerable center of her torso.

Natalya darted opposite the woman's twist, plunging a third dagger into the wide expanse of her back.

Her screech echoed out into the night.

The door to the officers' quarters slammed open, and a trio of men stormed out onto the deck.

A muffled shout rose up from below but quickly fell silent.

Natalya called another dagger, cursing herself for not asking enough questions when Tomas explained their mission, too distracted by whatever was preventing her from communicating with Piper within the noble's city manse. She'd run out before subduing all those on deck at this rate, and she'd only worn a couple of her blades for their trip to Nobles' Row.

"Aye! You!" The first of the three figures spied her in the center of the deck as the woman she'd been fighting tipped forward, collapsing onto the polished wooden surface, her blood a steadily spreading pool around her.

Natalya plucked the blade from the woman's back and let the other two go. They disappeared into the night's ether.

Serrana's newspapers had given her many names over the years—Invisible Weaponess among her favorites.

She searched the sides of the ship for the backup that was supposed to come to her aid should matters go awry. Where were they?

Randolf didn't usually order death on a first attempt at evading his demands, so this crew must be repeat offenders. Natalya had long suspected he enjoyed the game of seeing who might try to defy him and who would cave.

The three men rushed toward her.

She aimed for the two on either side first.

They tried to use the crates stacked along the ship's deck to protect themselves, dipping in and out of shadows and behind crates.

"It's the Blade!" one shouted, calling out the most common of her names known and feared by the sailors who docked in Serrana, raising the alarm across the ship and along the docks.

She silenced him with a dagger to the throat, screaming as the dagger left her fingertips. Where were Randolf and the others? Did he mean to let these sailors kill her?

"Just like he warned us!" a second cried, his silhouette emerging between two barrels. Natalya's thrown dagger brushed along the back of his shirt, half a breath behind impaling her mark.

"Gah!" A deep-throated cry rang out from the levy docks as a stream of hooded figures stormed up the gangplank. *Finally.*

A bevy of shouts and thumps echoed from below.

Natalya inched back toward the mast, careful of the

spilled blood slicking the polished decking, searching the shadows for the two sailors.

Was Tomas faring any better belowdecks? It would take their reinforcements longer to get to him below.

The heavy thud of booted steps cut short her fears for her friend as the second sailor rushed her. She flung her daggers freely, aiming for his throat, the hollows beneath his shoulders. The moment one magical blade left her grasp, she willed another into place.

With six daggers thrown, two of the three sailors slumped onto the deck. Spots of black pricked along the edges of Natalya's vision. She was expending her reserves too quickly and would run out before long.

The din of combat grew louder along the docks and the edges of the deck, with reserves from both sides answering the call to combat.

Something wasn't right. There were too many sailors nearby. Were the Tidings less trained in combat, they might be overwhelmed.

"Ar-agghh!" The hunched shape of the third burst out of the darkness, propelling himself toward her.

With a cry, Natalya mustered the last of her energy to conjure a thin blade in each hand.

She pierced the sailor through as he tackled her, sending them both rolling across the ship. He thumped back into one of the cargo boxes, eyes as wide as the first sailor's had been, his breath coming too quickly.

Her twin daggers poked out from beneath his ribs. This one was lucky—he might live.

The sailor looked from Natalya down to the daggers

and back. He made to remove one of the blades but she caught his hand. "Don't do that. You'll bleed out."

He nodded, the motion slight, and sat back against the wood, content to pant. "The nobleman warned us," he murmured to himself, staring back at Natalya in horror as though she were a ghost in the night. "Said the Blade would be here, hungry to take what was owed. Shoulda listened."

Too late, Natalya raised a hand to her hood. It had fallen back when he tackled her. The moonlight brightened her already white hair and cast a lilac hue across her pale skin.

By the shadows, Natalya cursed to herself. Whatever his rank among the crew, this sailor would pay with his life for seeing her face.

Even though Randolf was angry with her, when it came to threats from without, the Tidings looked after their own.

"Who warned you we'd be here? Which nobleman?" Natalya demanded, tugging the dagger out of her gauntlet and holding it to the man's throat.

The sailor smiled at her desperation, a dreamy expression coming over his face. "It was just like the priestess said. His priestess, the nobleman."

He was losing blood quickly, the coherence ebbing out with each pulse of his heart.

Randolf would lock her away again if he learned she'd been this close to discovering who had tipped the crew off about the Tidings' visit and still failed to capture the name. The sailor's head thumped back against the wood of the mast.

"I need the name." Natalya leaned closer. "It's not too late for you," she bargained. "You'll live. But I need the informant's name."

"Whatssit, Blade?" One of Randolf's largest and most trusted hands hovered behind her, a brother-at-arms at his side.

"Are you playing with your food, Nata?" the other asked, Piper's nickname for her a twisting dagger in her gut.

She ignored them and returned her focus to the sailor. "We can get you to the healers, but you have to answer me. Who warned you?"

The sailor shuddered beneath the intensity of her stare, his gaze darting about. He drew in a low, panicked gasp as stillness settled over the docks and lapped across the deck.

She would know the rhythm of those boot-steps anywhere. Randolf approached. "You've completed your task just in time, little blade," the leader of the Tidings said, his voice a warm swell behind her, praise and something else she couldn't gauge lingering on his voice.

It was the first time he'd addressed her openly in weeks.

After her visit to see Piper at Atkinson's estate, she'd confronted Randolf about Piper's suspicions, demanding to be sure that he wasn't targeting and trying to ruin her sister. She'd wanted to know the extent of his involvement with Lord Atkinson's affairs.

Randolf's hurt at her distrust quickly spiraled into rage. He hurled accusations of his own that Natalya was little better than her sister, siding with the nobles and their ilk rather than with the cause she'd professed to be working toward for years.

"There's a fine line between ideals and survival," she'd thrown back at Randolf, too angry herself to adequately gauge his emotions.

His mouth a compressed line, he'd locked her away.

Three days in the cells, a different interrogator every few hours.

He'd sent Tomas to free her, her release coming after Atkinson relocated himself and Piper into the merchants' district, making it harder for Natalya to visit Piper without drawing suspicion. Unlike the nobles' quarter, the merchants' streets were always bustling.

The corruption Piper had suspected, that Natalya had sworn the Tidings were innocent of, came flooding back to her.

She stiffened, making the sailor gasp as the dagger she held pierced his skin. Her magical blades spent, the dagger from her gauntlet had been the nearest at hand to subdue the sailor.

Cursing the effect Randolf had over her concentration, Natalya withdrew the point of her blade from the man's throat and turned to regard the Tidings' leader, his hat shading his face from the light of the moons.

"The sailors said they knew to expect us. Whose cargo is this?" Her voice was cold, slightly hoarse. After what he'd put her through in the cells, while the possibility remained that he'd been lying to her all along, she could hardly bring herself to address him at all.

"Mine," Randolf growled.

Natalya's hand shook as she tightened her grip on

the hilt. "Whose was it before?" She scanned the crates behind Randolf, searching for a name. Port of destination, port of arrival.

"A noble's."

"Which. One," Natalya demanded.

But the leader of the Tidings only smiled. "One who, after crossing me, is no more." Randolf's voice dropped an octave as he spoke, but Natalya couldn't deny the suspicion that had swept over her with the sailor's fear. "We have been through this already, and as you've worked out, there's a rat in our ranks."

Overhead, the wind whipped at the rigging, punctuating the night with the billow of fabric, its metal ties clanging as they struck the solid beam of the mast.

"That's why you locked me away. And yet the sailors still knew to expect us. *Why?*" Natalya urged the beat of her heart to slow, her hand to hold steady. The subdued sailor might turn on her at any moment.

With a nod, Randolf signaled to one of his men behind her to close in. She'd be trapped within moments, and it wouldn't matter if Randolf confirmed that he had been behind Atkinson's death. He could have even confessed to collusion with the very nobles he professed to despise—pinned aboard and outnumbered, she'd never be able to get away to help Piper.

Natalya whirled around to the sailor held fast at the point of her blade. "Who do you sail for? Who owns your merchants?"

Randolf had taught her the order of things long ago. Merchants owned sailors. Nobles owned merchants and courtesans. There were only two ways to opt out of the hierarchy—sell yourself to Gaia and the priestesses, or be owned by a band of thieves.

She'd chosen the latter, seeing no other option at the time. Had she doomed Piper in her selection? Betrayed her loyalty to her sister in siding with the Tidings?

"Lord Atkinson," the soldier croaked, eyes widening as he looked over Natalya's shoulder. "Before he died, and now—"

"Do it," Randolf ordered.

A thick boot stomped down beside Natalya alongside the ring and thud of steel.

The pinned sailor gargled, choking around the blade that pierced through his throat. His blood gurgled out of the wound, sopping his shirt. A shining bib of black in the night, reflecting the light of the moons.

"Did you really think you and your sister could escape my web, little blade? That I wouldn't know of your secret rendezvous to spy on Piper's new Suzerain this afternoon?" He tilted his head to the side, that same hurt from before catching in his voice. "Is Oxbrow trying to turn you against me?" Yet another accusation leveled at her, though this one rang false, like Randolf was listing it out of obligation rather than belief.

Natalya's lips parted, suddenly lost in Randolf's mix of paranoia and bluster. The expression she'd sensed before but hadn't understood fell into place—fear. Her thoughts skipped ahead, angling the pieces into a pattern. This nobleman who held her sister had something over Randolf too, some threat he couldn't abide. The leader of the Tidings wasn't as independent as he'd always claimed, and whatever his new entrapment was with Oxbrow, it made him dangerous. Untrustworthy and untrusting. She wasn't sure which was worse. Either way, she had to get to Piper, protect her from Randolf's coming wrath. He'd never assent to a noble's control of his holdings, even if he had to destroy those he'd sworn to help in the process.

Randolf stomped closer. "Whatever lies he's spun for your sister and she, in turn, has wrapped around you, never forget—the city is mine. *You* are mine. I won't have you hung over my head to keep me in line in some noble-man's scheme. Don't think you can fool me, little blade. Choose your next steps carefully."

Natalya bunched her hands into fists. No magical knives answered. Her chest rose and fell quickly with her breath. If she threw the blade in hand, she'd only have the ones in her boots and other gauntlet left. Not enough to fend off the Tidings.

What tangled web had Randolf found himself trapped within, between Atkinson and Oxbrow, and somehow involving herself and Piper? "Is he why you locked me away before?"

"Hah," Randolf barked, his laugh ringing falsely against the stillness of the night. "As though a noble's idle threats could force my hand." Behind her, the other Tidings shifted nervously, waiting for their leader to rein in his command.

He leveled his gaze with her. "But I had to be sure. Had to know I could still trust you."

His partial confession nestled uneasily with Natalya's understanding of the Tidings' position within Serrana and the accusations Piper had first made on behalf of her

Suzerain. There was some hand, a will manipulating Randolf's actions, toward an end she still couldn't work out.

What she *did* know was Randolf's tactics—he'd planned this confrontation following a fight specifically, urging her into danger so that when the two of them faced off, she'd be less of a threat.

Hands still shaking, Natalya rose. She held Randolf's gaze. "If it's trust we're after, I'll ask *you* one final time— Were you behind Atkinson's ruin? Were you backing Oxbrow against him? Putting up Piper as . . . collateral?" The idea was so disgusting, so entirely possible, especially if Randolf believed Oxbrow could threaten his position within the city, she could barely speak the words aloud.

Randolf shook his head. "I told you the order of things, little blade." He ran his tongue over his front teeth, his mouth making a sucking sound as he rolled his shoulders back. "Told you the truth then and again now. The day I get in bed with a merchant and start whoring myself like your sister is the day I lose the reputation I've so carefully built. The day I lose all those who put their faith in me."

She had no words, only hatred and despair burbling up into her throat, stealing her voice.

Randolf crossed his arms over his bulging chest, watching her carefully. "Your sister's nobleman put his trust in a snake, but that's a mistake you and I won't make." A glimmer of moonlight caught in his eye. "We can make him pay."

Finally, a ring of truth. "You had an agreement with

him already, one that ruined Atkinson and led to his death, to Piper's *imprisonment*." All movement around them ceased, and murmurs rose up among the Tidings. They'd known Piper as long as they'd known Natalya. Her passion and kindness had made her a favorite among them early on, her presence suffused with a warmth Natalya would never possess. She had to win others over in her own way, one that took more time and usually involved her blades.

Randolf stretched his jaw to the side, making her believe, just for a moment, that he truly felt sorrow for what had befallen Piper, for the predations of the wider world. "What you're accusing me of still—you take too simple a view of our world, little blade. I tried to teach you better than that."

The lack of denial was enough of a confession for her.

Natalya clenched her teeth and tightened her arms against her ribcage. She was tired of being told what her place should be. "You taught me plenty." Natalya flung the blade from her hand to strike just below Randolf's collarbone, sending him flying back with a roar.

It wouldn't be enough to kill him. She couldn't handle that.

He'd taught her what to do when penned—fight like you can't count on anyone else save yourself. And he'd just shown her how little she could count on him to help her or save Piper.

Be practical, he'd liked to say. She was, now. He'd given her no choice. When she freed Piper from the noble, she'd need an ordered world in which to make their escape.

Randolf was the steady center that bound the fateful ropes of Serrana together.

Natalya leapt for the gangway and slid quickly out of the grasp of her former allies' flying frames, grabbing at her.

"Stop her!" Randolf cried, a strange desperation clinging to his voice. "Natalya, you don't understand!"

She ignored her former mentor's plea and sprinted for the one place she knew she could make her escape and ensure Piper's as well. The stench of the sewers opened wide to meet her. With a final deep breath of untainted air, Natalya plunged inside.

The Tidings—her former friends—stormed after her. Their wet, thumping steps echoed all around the sewers, drowning out any other warning sound.

With years of service to Randolf, Natalya knew these tunnels as well as she knew the paths through the trees of the forest where she and Piper had grown up. She could find her way through the dark, scale the fence of Oxbrow's estate, and rescue her sister, using the sewers again to make their escape before daybreak.

We'll be back in the forest, back home, *in a matter of days*, Natalya repeated to herself in the moments when the sewers' stench nearly overwhelmed her, burning her eyes, making her gag.

The disturbance upon the docks had prevented her from bidding farewell to Tomas, but he would know better than to come after her. As fond of her and Piper as he was, not even Tomas would brave the depths of the forest the city-dwellers thought was haunted. The urban priestesses had done little to disabuse them of such notions, which meant she and Piper would be safe from pursuit as soon as they gained the forest's borders.

Contracting Piper as a dancer and courtesan and Natalya as an assassin wasn't a favor Randolf had done out of the goodness of his heart, Natalya reminded herself, finding a greater burst of speed and increasing the distance from her pursuers with each stride.

"Cut her off!" "Head around that way!"

They were many and she was one. They knew where she was going.

Natalya tucked her chin and ran like her sister's life depended on it.

Because deep down, she knew it did.

Even deeper, an ancient sense, passed down to her through the generations, reminded her of yet another option before her, a way to escape them where they'd never outpace her, and even if they found her, they'd never survive.

No, Natalya pushed back against that ancient knowing. *Not the wolf.* Her family had survived Eamon's curse for this long. She wouldn't give in to it now.

Natalya gripped the wolf's head ring upon her finger, reassuring herself of its steady, soothing presence there. It allowed her to remain who she truly was. A fae. Nothing more.

She tucked herself tightly around a narrow corner, stooping to keep the grime of the low tunnel from her hair. The men Randolf had sent after her would have to crouch and pursue in single file. She covered her nose and swallowed a choking gag as her boot squelched into a pile of refuse. Piper would do this and more for her.

To push away her ancestors' promise of aid, she turned her spinning thoughts to Randolf's hand in their current predicament instead. There was more to his dispassionate reaction to Piper's imprisonment with her new Suzerain than he was letting on. Why had he brought up Oxbrow by name just now, believing that wretch had somehow influenced Natalya?

She knew as well as Randolf that Piper's connection to the nobles made her a valuable asset. Why would he have been willing to let that go?

Natalya clenched her jaw, redirecting her energy to the task at hand. There were pursuers behind, her sister in danger ahead.

She grabbed the edges of her hood and tugged it over her hair. A blade in the darkness. She cut through the sewers, her destination clear in her mind. On the other side of the tunnels, Piper was waiting.

CHAPTER 6
NATALYA

At the top of Nobles' Row, the storm drains washed down into the lower sewers, their entrances hidden by artfully designed twisting hollows crafted by the city's earthshapers, those gifted with earthen magic but separate from the priestesses of Gaia.

Pressing her hand against dirt rather than stone, Natalya felt a glimmer of energy return, though the rigors of the night's attacks weighed on her, and she was no closer to understanding Randolf's sudden desperation, the random bite of his actions.

The city watch patrolled Nobles' Row on horseback, sitting tall, clomping by in bobbing pairs, the curling *H* of the duke's crest spread across their chests.

They glanced to the sides as they rode past, secure in their high position and in the quiet of the street, unaware of what lurked in the shadows. The murmur of their conversation fell away, followed by the fading clack of their horses' hooves upon the cobbles. Natalya darted from the waterway across the street, dipping quickly past the elegant mansions of the city's nobility, slowing as she reached Oxbrow's manse.

The wolf in Natalya's blood, the wild manifestation of her inheritance, paced along the edges of her mind, its attention divided by the sense of danger around her that had already swallowed her sister and the magical ring on her finger that held it at bay.

Against her own instincts—those she had cultivated rather than those she had been cursed with since birth—Natalya slowed her slinking progress as she neared Oxbrow's manse. The Tidings would be close on her heels, but being caught by her own was a far kinder fate than whatever waited behind Oxbrow's walls.

Natalya kept her low position, slinking forward and darting into the shadows of Oxbrow's tall, iron-barred walls, their spears punctuated by columns of stone. Unlike the delicate gardens and impractically whimsical architecture favored by the rest of Serrana, Oxbrow's manse glared brutishly down from its position in the center of Nobles' Row, a scarred, scowling warrior within a traipsing troupe of courtiers.

Cutting shadows across the grass, uniformed guards circled the estate, weaving about the grounds in overlapping routes. Depending on the path she chose, her luck, and her timing, these concentric patterns might work to her advantage. Was the logic of patrolling the center of the estate to ensure no one from inside escaped just as much as preventing an outsider from gaining entry?

Thick clouds rolled over the greater moon, leaving only the sliver of the lesser. The nights were growing shorter as winter gave way to spring. In less than an hour, the first rays of dawn would peek over the forest that bordered the city, holding all the noise and inhabitants inside.

Further down the pebbled walk, near where she and Tomas had crouched that morning, hushed voices disrupted the stillness of the nobles' street.

From within the estate's grounds, a shrill whistle rent the air.

Natalya grinned. The Tidings pursuing her had provided the perfect distraction for her to scale the fence and cross the estate grounds.

Outside the gate where the guard had confronted her and Tomas, one hulking, dark-clad figure shoved another. "You've given us away."

"Eh! They're back!" one of the guards shouted from within the fence, his voice echoing just as loudly as his whistled call of distress.

As other guards took up the first's cry, stomping across the grounds as fast as they could to offer assistance in subduing the growing number of the Tidings pouring out of the sewers, Natalya rolled her shoulders back and leapt for the iron bars, her right hand reaching as high as she could, swinging up higher with her left and catching the crossbeam along the top of the fencing.

She perched at the top, surveying her best path across the grounds, and leapt for the grassy knoll beneath. A rolling tumble sent her springing onto her feet and into a crouched sprint across the expansive estate.

The guards' interrupted patrols allowed her to steal into the green-walled garden abutting the estate with no one to hear the crunch of her boots upon the gravel pathways.

The heights of the garden's hedges would have given the sense of being trapped in a strangely large maze were it not for the looming shape of the manse overhead, guiding Natalya's way through patches of rambling roses hacked back into oddly squared shapes, the once-graceful forms of trees shorn too close to the trunk, making them appear shriveled and more vulnerable to storms. The combined effect of the urban gardening served to diminish the natural, earthen lines, subduing the greenery to echo the harsh shape of the manse instead.

Nearer to the house, the maze gave way to a series of gravel paths, one of which curved around the side of the manse where a narrow stairwell yawned open into the darkness.

Natalya leapt down the stairs three at a time.

She stabbed the guard she encountered at the base of the stairs through the throat, damaging the dagger from her opposite bracer.

The keys from his belt opened the side door and a long dungeon hallway where slivers of moonlight illuminated row upon row of cages. Some were occupied but most were empty.

Only a few of the prisoners looked up, most of them too beaten down to respond to a shift in their environment. Were her standing with the Tidings different, this was precisely the sort of excess that she could report to

Randolf, which he would then order the Tidings to avenge and stop.

At the center of the cages was an open square of planed gray rock, a hole cut in the center of the blood-stained floor.

A drain, Natalya realized as she rushed past, chills prickling over her skin.

The buzzing she'd sensed from the estate's borders whined in her ears, dulling her sense of her surroundings. But she pressed on.

On the opposite end of the dungeons from where she'd entered, a curling stairwell led out into the main house.

She'd tracked the interior movements as best she could. The kitchens and the endlessly specific chambers that nobles kept for varying inane purposes lay on one end of the house. The residences were at the other.

Natalya crept down the corridor, her steps muted by the plush carpets underneath, one of many luxuries missing from the home where she'd last visited Piper.

No servants waited at the base of the stairs. No steward questioned her place of origin. No guards waited outside closed-off chambers.

The house was still and silent.

The light click of her footfalls sounded across the carved marble staircase as Natalya hurried up to the second floor. By the shadows, this hallway was even longer than the one in Atkinson's home. More doorways than Ackley kept for paying clients in the upstairs of La Consagrada stretched before Natalya.

How was she ever to locate which was Piper's room

in a space that the entirety of the Tidings and their relatives would struggle to fill?

Think like a noble. The grandest place to be is likely also the least convenient and the best for show.

The end of the hall, furthest from the servants and the kitchens to maximize inconvenience.

Natalya nodded to herself and hurried forward, confident in her assessment of the manse's layout, creeping along the center of the long carpet, darting through the windows of moonlight that shone along the hall.

There wasn't time for indecision.

At the hall's end, the architecture widened into a circle, the offset branch of towers visible from the outside. Three doors, with arched windows between them which bathed the rounded corridor in pale light.

Natalya paused, trying to discern which might belong to Piper.

Had there been guards posted outside one of the doors, she would have had a better clue.

With nothing to go on, Natalya decided to start with the door on the left. She stole into the open, moonlight washing over her.

The crackling strike of a match cast ice across her heart. With the match came a flare of fire in the dark, illuminating a shadowed figure leaning against the wall, hidden by the opulent pillars of the doorframe.

"It is awfully late for callers," the figure observed, his voice whining and unpleasant.

Natalya froze within the entry to the rounded portion of the hall. If she ran now, she might be able to leap over the banister by the stairs and make her escape, but doing so would mean leaving Piper behind.

She angled her shoulders toward the noble instead. He was much smaller than the thieves she sparred with, practicing for confrontations precisely like this one in the basement of La Consagrada.

A second figure peeled itself off the wall, following the first. Natalya cursed under her breath at having missed them both. She should have sensed them. Something about the magic that permeated this house set her teeth on edge.

"You know as well as I that the Blade keeps irregular hours, Oxbrow," the second figure answered.

With practiced ease, Natalya adjusted her stance to account for there being two opponents rather than one.

"Did you not wonder at so easily gaining the house?" the man with the nasal voice said, tilting his head in mockery. He puffed on his tobacco roll. The second watched her, far warier than his accomplice. "Do you believe me so weak and ineffectual—like all the others you and your sister insist on surrounding yourselves with—that I'm incapable of defending my own house from a common bandit?" His questions set his temper on edge, sent him stomping toward Natalya.

The second man caught him by the elbow before he could pass within her reach. "Felix," he warned.

Natalya narrowed her gaze. This second noble was the one to watch, the true danger, and the one in control here.

"I must say," Oxbrow taunted, leaning toward her while the other man restrained him by the arm, "you were slower to come to your sister's rescue than I would have expected."

"Piper?" Natalya sent out into the darkness. From what she knew of nobles' homes, she should be near the courtiers' residences. In other cases, if she desired to speak within someone else's mind, she had to see them, but Natalya had kept her ability secret from anyone they'd met in Serrana save Tomas. Her connection with Piper was special. Before her sister's imprisonment, it had acted at Natalya's will, Piper's voice as common a companion to her thoughts as her own.

It had taken a great deal of concentration to shield Piper from the knowledge of Natalya's confrontation with Randolf, the days locked away, hiding her pain and distraction from her sister's steady drip of the details of packing and relocating house.

"Have you worked out the clamping of the vice around your ankles yet? The careful arranging of events beyond your control to lead you precisely here?"

"Felix . . ." the second figure warned again.

Oxbrow dragged greedily from his tobacco roll. "I didn't expect you to be clever enough to see it, though I expected Randolf to put up more of a fight to shield his holdings and you from what had to be done."

They had passed the point of it mattering whether or not Oxbrow was telling the truth. She needed to get past these two, now, get Piper, and leave.

Natalya dipped her chin and reached to withdraw the knife from her boot.

"Not a movement further," the second man warned, his free hand extended toward her. He gave a quick whistle. All along the hall, doors opened. Broad-chested guards sidled out of their hiding places.

Where they'd been lying in wait.

Just like the sailors had known she would be.

Hopelessly outnumbered, her options grew thin. Had Randolf been trying to prevent her arrival here or urged her toward this outcome? Her hands trembled at the thought, but at least someone knew where she was. The whole of the Tidings knew where she'd gone. They would come for her.

Too late, Natalya remembered the blade she'd tossed into Randolf's shoulder, the reason she only had the boot blades remaining.

'Choose carefully,' Randolf had always said. She never could have killed him. Hurting him was hard enough, but he'd recover.

The choice was the same one she'd made every day in the streets of Serrana. The choice that had led them to Randolf. Piper. Always.

Natalya straightened, calling upon the dregs of her magic to serve her this one last time. If she could conjure the blades, could strike at these nobles, holding their lives over the guards' heads, she and Piper might be able to make their escape.

"Piper?" Natalya shouted. She called her sister's name a second time, without answer.

Oxbrow's sneer twisted into an unsightly grin.

Something was desperately wrong within this house, with this nobleman. She sensed it in the unease of the second, how he was almost equally wary of Oxbrow and her.

Please, just this once—

She willed the blades to appear.

A tremble raced up her spine.

She had one option remaining. The curse that had lingered in her blood since birth, that had sent her mother away with Natalya's coming of age.

"Crow all you want," Natalya answered the nobleman's taunts, the low scratch of her voice making Oxbrow startle back. She smirked. "Unless you release my sister into my care, now, my eyes will be the last thing you ever see."

"Hah!" the pale nobleman cried.

Natalya reached for the ring upon her thumb, ready to unleash the wolf who dwelled within.

The second nobleman yanked Oxbrow back. He bobbed his chin, signaling over Natalya's shoulder. "Now!" he called.

A sharp sting shot into the back of her neck. Natalya winced, reaching back for the dart.

"Told you she'd put up a fight."

"A good sign."

The voices blurred as the world slid into darkness.

No, she was sliding toward the floor, dart in hand.

Polished leather shoes without a speck of dirt or wear blocked Natalya's view of her surroundings, the pale leather dully reflecting the moonlight pouring in from the windows and casting clouds across her vision.

She willed her feet to move. Her head. Her body didn't respond. The shoes slid closer.

Natalya honed her focus, collapsing her will to survive, to save Piper into a last stand.

Her hand held the pointed dart with a narrow, needle-point tip.

She tightened her grasp and raised her hand an inch from the ground. It moved.

With all her might, she stabbed the dart into the shoe, piercing through the leather and striking into flesh.

The man screamed, stumbling back before crashing onto the ground.

Natalya smiled to herself as the darkness claimed her.

CHAPTER 7

TOMAS

TEN DAYS LATER

Tomas paced before Randolf's desk, having held his peace for long enough—almost a day and a half this time—before renewing his plea that the Tidings either raid or raze Oxbrow's manor house and extract Piper and Natalya from it.

"You know Natalya would do that and more for either of us," Tomas added, brightening at this clever new twist to his speech, one he hadn't thought of before.

Randolf's jaw jutted forward as the leader of the Tidings rubbed his chest just beneath where Natalya's blade had struck him the night she made her escape to rescue Piper.

No one had caught sight of her since.

"I am not sure your assessment is true, at least not in my case," Randolf said, his voice betraying no sense of his internal state, though that wasn't unusual.

"It was just a misunderstanding between the two of

you," Tomas reasoned. He counted himself among the more sensitive of the Tidings—something he had been hoping Natalya would notice and appreciate about him before long—and he knew that her absence bothered Randolf just as much if not more than it did him.

Since Natalya's disappearance, Randolf's temper had been even shorter than usual, flaring at the most unlikely triggers—anything, Tomas suspected, that reminded him of Natalya.

"She didn't know about your concerns that we'd lose our station in the docks, the threat you were under. Or about this other figure . . ." He slowed his explanation at the careful narrowing of Randolf's gaze.

"And which other figure might you be referring to, Tomas?"

"Erm, well, Oxbrow. The one who came here to make demands just before we lost Natalya." He hastily wiped at the bead of sweat that had appeared along his brow.

Randolf smirked as though he could read Tomas's thoughts. "And where else have you picked up this suspicion?"

Tomas bit his lower lip. Maybe he had gone too far this time, but it really wasn't right for them to leave Natalya to fend for herself, so he'd taken some precautions, just a few, enough that he could continue his regular work with as little interruption as possible.

His leader's unwavering stare bore into his thoughts.

He dropped his head. "F-from the urchins I paid to stand watch along the borders of the estate. In case she steps outside or tries to get a signal to us of what kind of help she needs. Where she is."

Randolf nodded, a slight twinge at the corner of his mouth with this revelation. "You mean you're paying orphans to keep a lookout, rather like how you came into my care in the first place?"

Tomas grinned at that. "Exactly, sir."

A dangerously serious expression passed over Randolf's features, like a sheet of rain washing over the docks. "I want you to listen to me very carefully, Tomas, as more lives than your own hang in the balance."

The side of Randolf's jaw tightened as though he was fighting to say and swallow his next words at once. "You have to let her go. That's what this comes down to."

Randolf slumped back in his seat. "She made her choice. But she's beyond our help now."

At first he thought he was misunderstanding. This was Natalya they were talking about, not a thug Randolf had pulled in off the street a few days before. She'd served the Tidings loyally for years.

But the pallor that had crept over Randolf's features, the stillness that hovered heavy upon his shoulders, served only to fan Tomas's fears.

Randolf wasn't going to help her. He'd have to find a way on his own.

CHAPTER 8

PIPER

"My sister will come for me," Piper promised Oxbrow when he finally appeared at the door of her prison. "She'll end you." She had turned her back before she waited to see if his expression changed, if he registered the desperate hope and utter terror in her threat.

Natalya was coming for her, she knew that. But whether they would both survive the attempted rescue was another matter.

Only when Oxbrow had stomped away, the tower door slamming shut behind him, did Piper add for herself what she most needed to hear, "I'm not alone."

She drummed her fingertips against the ornate emerald collar Oxbrow had presented upon her arrival, insisting that, as his newest jewel, she be the one to bear it. The extravagance of the gift had rendered her speechless, emeralds being the most valuable jewels in all of Draykemire, treasured for their connection to the titan of earth, Gaia, the one to whom the priestesses of the Serra Valley pledged their lives and service.

The necklace was the one kindness she'd received since joining Oxbrow's household.

Fingers tapping a half-remembered melody across the gemstones, Piper thought over and over of the visions she and her mother had shared, visions that had left no room for doubt—the girls made their way in Serrana, became courtesans. Natalya would find a home within a castle, her equal by her side.

Before Mamaun left them, her ring passed down to Natalya, Piper had asked her why she never saw herself in the recurring vision.

Mamaun had paled. "Even for those blessed as we are, there's only so much we can see as we look ahead." Their mother had returned to the Shadowlands shortly thereafter, hoping to find the daimon of Verrain before the empress's guards found her. The ring she'd entrusted to Natalya prevented her sister's transformations into a daimon wolf, the part of their blood inheritance that had sparked their grandmother's flight from the Shadowlands in the first place. The empress had ordered them to be hunted to extinction.

The girls had never discovered whether or not Mamaun had been successful, whether or not she'd survived.

Weeks passed into months of Piper's imprisonment within Oxbrow's rooms. Some days there were questions. Some days tests of blood, experiments, with the vials and needles that rested against the wall, watching her always.

And then one day, something shifted. Oxbrow stormed into her chamber, his patience already thin. A handful of unknown guards accompanied him.

He asked a series of strange questions about her family's origin. Oxbrow demanded answers she'd promised to keep secret and others she didn't know. She lied until she believed her stories as new truths. Whatever it took to protect Natalya. He couldn't learn who she really was. What she was capable of. The magic that ran in their veins.

This wasn't the first of Oxbrow's interrogations where she'd been beaten, and through the beginning, she assumed it wouldn't be the last. "Do it," Oxbrow ordered the head of his guard, who stepped forward from the wall and stood behind Piper's huddled form on the floor.

He wrapped his hand around the emerald choker, the one he'd insisted she keep through her imprisonment within the tower bedroom despite depriving her of all other signs of her rank.

Piper choked, her eyes bulging, as the guard lifted her off the ground, holding her aloft by the emeralds around her neck. She sputtered, clawed at her throat as stars danced along the corners of her eyes.

"You swore your sister would come for you," Oxbrow seethed. "She hasn't and she won't. She's abandoned you, so why sacrifice your own life to protect one so selfish, someone who's proven her lack of regard again and again?"

Tears streamed from the corners of Piper's eyes. She could scarcely hear Oxbrow's threats in his wretched nasal voice over her own gagging, her desperation for breath.

She struck out to kick the guard behind her, but he barely reacted to her assault. At Oxbrow's order, two others came to join the first guard, pinning her arms to her sides and holding her feet bound.

The stars began to obscure her vision, the world turning to darkness.

"What does your sister keep hidden from the empress of Verrain?" Oxbrow screeched, desperation driving his voice an octave higher. "Tell me!"

With Oxbrow's question, Piper's thoughts turned to Natalya, the vision she'd seen of her sister's happiness, promised by the fates. For herself, she'd been wrong about the dream she'd cherished for her entire life. She'd thought she would find her dream's fulfillment with a Suzerain—a deep, overwhelming love and partnership.

Piper stopped struggling, relaxing into the emeralds' choking hold.

That love and partnership, she'd had all along, since birth, her first memories being of Natalya, only a little taller than she was, trying to protect her from the outside world.

Piper released her final breath, imagining Natalya by her side as she'd been for so long. As they would have stayed, had she and Mamaun given Natalya her way instead of insisting on what the fates had laid out for them.

She didn't hear the guards struggling in the hallway, their fight to subdue a prisoner they'd brought up from the manse's dungeons, brought into the light for the first time in months.

The guards in the hall would have stood a better chance if those inside hadn't opened the door when they did, giving the prisoner a perfect view of what had transpired within the round chamber.

From just outside the doorway, the prisoner's enraged scream echoed down Oxbrow's halls, reverberating out to the streets beyond. The already struggling guards cried out in alarm and immediately fell silent, a gurgle of blood and the hiss of a magical blade severing their tether to the world.

The lavender daggers flew about the hall, into the round stone chamber.

Oxbrow screamed, attempting to shield himself with his guards' bodies as one and the next slumped to the floor, the glow of amethyst runes and lilac blades shimmering against the blood that pulsed out of their wounds.

NATALYA

In a storm of daggers that flew as feathers, Natalya was there, just as Piper had known she would be.

The runes' text had been determined long ago, in the heart of the Shadowlands, where a fae fought for those she loved—*Pain and blood mark the path to Vengeance.*

The blades slowed, and Natalya bellowed her sister's name as she fought the unending sea of guards, growing only more desperate when Piper still did not answer her.

Alongside her shouts for Piper, Natalya repeated to herself, to her sister's spirit, what their mother had taught them in the forest so long ago. *To the shadows.*

She collapsed a guard's windpipe with a blow from her elbow. Plunged another's broken ribs into the wet hollows of his lungs.

To the shadows.

Gouged out eyes. Clawed at throats. Dodged blows.

To the shadows.

However many fell, more came. They were nothing more than obstacles, keeping her from the still form draped across the center of the room, an emerald choker gleaming around her throat.

Piper's lips were blue. Her dark hair had fallen from its ties. Shadows hung beneath closed lids that covered beloved, coppery eyes.

Natalya's breaths came in gasps.

"Piper—"

Silence answered.

"Piper—"

A sea of hands seized her. Shouted about a syringe.

"Piper . . ."

To my revenge.

CHAPTER 9
OXBROW

L ord Felix Oxbrow dabbed at the crust of sweat that had formed at the top of his neckerchief, leaning away from the overly stuffed armchair either Amelia or Cecilia—who could recall which?—had insisted he would find a great luxury behind his desk. He'd been searching for a way out of a quarrel with the other twin at the time and hadn't objected to the supreme discomfort provoked by the chair's arms rising to equal height with the desk itself, pinning him in at an uncomfortable distance from his ledger like a child who had too quickly gained admittance to adult dining spaces.

He sighed his displeasure through his nose and tried once more to turn his attention to the stack of urgent documents brought by his steward. Ledgers, reports of the Tidings' movements, rumors of similar organizations trying to sidle into the resultant power vacuum now that Randolf had been brought to heel.

Oxbrow clicked his tongue behind his teeth. Defeat will do that to a person. It was a victory he still savored.

Near the bottom of the stack, an inconspicuously dull-looking document revealed itself to be a clipping from the gossip magazine of Sanctuary's social set—a piece about the queen's harvest festival, hosted by her city every three years in celebration of Draykemire's peace and a symbol of unity between herself and her brothers. Twenty years, the longest the Orbaskier line had ever gone without open conflict between their members.

Oxbrow skimmed the piece, finding nothing of interest to himself until, finally, he discovered why his steward had ensured he saw the article in the first place. The gossip columnist listed the eligible bachelors planning to attend the harvest festival so that those fascinated by the nobility might participate in a matchmaking betting contest for those not of the courtier or noble set.

Near the top of the list—unpleasantly, a few rows above himself; he would lodge a complaint later—Felix spied one name in particular, Lord Silas Graveston, of Hillearst. His arch rival. Silas had been disappointingly absent from the festival three years prior, but this year, Felix would more than make up for Graveston's absence then.

He glared out the window, recalling all the unpleasant encounters they'd had before. Graveston believed himself to be everything Felix wasn't—restrained, a man of action, principled.

Felix's lip curled. To see the look upon Graveston's face when he first spied the emerald collar, plucked from the neck of Graveston's unfortunate, now mad aunt. *A trophy upon a trophy.* Natalya would make the perfect puppet upon which to display his double victory.

He'd settled the matter of losing one of the Slip-shayde sisters well enough, though his benefactors had been painfully clear as to what a second such slip-up would cost.

Oxbrow tossed back the finger of brandy that remained in his glass. If only that were enough to drown out the memory of the mage's demonstration of power.

The blood trials were getting nearer each day, he reminded himself. Soon, he and his poisoner would succeed in distilling the magic of Natalya's bloodline into a sample that could be sent to the empress of Verrain, securing her favor.

The following steps were simple—gift a secret vial of whatever the magic was to Queen Alsea and let the two sovereigns battle for control of their regions across both the Shadowlands and Eldura. From their kingdom's ashes, the earl would rise to power, Oxbrow at his side.

He tossed his hair back, imagining the adoring crowds throwing flowers and coins at his feet. The wealth he'd gain as head of the new king's accounts—he would own Draykemire in all but name and, come to think of it, even a throne could be bought.

Felix wriggled his shoulders against the stuffing once

more, returning his attention to the rival negata who believed himself so loyal, of such service to his duke.

Heh. The truest loyalty was to oneself.

He'd ensure Lord Silas Graveston understood as much before the end. But first, there was his rival's humiliation at the harvest festival celebration to arrange.

A muffled knock came from outside his study. "Come in," Oxbrow drawled.

His steward was there, looking strained.

Felix motioned the man inside. Spying the scarlet borders of the cream parchment upon his steward's silver tray, he understood the cause for concern. "Tell me," Felix ordered. "I know you've read it."

The steward slid into the office and shut the door behind him. He lifted the parchment. "Ahem. There has been a development," the steward read aloud, careful to keep his voice low despite the cushioning of the musty room full of books—the perfect noise dampeners, however dull they otherwise proved to be.

Trust the earl to begin with something so vague as to be entirely unhelpful.

"You must prepare," the steward continued. "We are no longer waiting on the empress. Make your move during the festival."

Oxbrow's eyes widened at the earl's orders. So matters were finally advancing despite the delay with the blood trials—his plan coming into being.

"One last thing, my lord," his steward added, "he says that the development entails a final necessity. There will be a three day delay, by order of the priestess."

"By *what*?" Oxbrow tried to spring out of his chair, catching his thighs against the edge of the desk instead.

He winced, falling back. Was the earl insane too? Missing the beginning of the festival would be near to a declaration of secession to Queen Alsea, which was tantamount to a declaration of war.

"Did the priestess add anything else?" he demanded. "Some explanation as to *why* such a step is necessary?" He pushed against the chair's heavy lower frame, finally extricating himself from beneath his desk. Where had he put that decanter of brandy?

"No, my lord." His steward lifted the card, showing Oxbrow the blank back of the parchment. "That is the end of his note."

"Very well," Oxbrow grumbled, stomping toward the door and taking the proffered parchment from the steward instead. "I'll see this burned."

Felix stormed down the hall, retracing his steps from that morning back toward his rooms, though he would first have to stop by the stone residence that abutted his. The fae had been growing restless within her tower prison, adapting to the sedatives while her blood resisted their trials.

His rivalry with Lord Graveston could wait a few days more. He pictured again the simmering rage upon the negata's face—and Natalya there to bear the brunt of Graveston's wrath.

Oxbrow chuckled to himself as he realized something the fae and Graveston had in common—a promise of revenge against him, and each of their plots doomed to failure. *Heh.* Perhaps this would be his most enjoyable harvest festival yet.

See you in Sanctuary, Graveston. Just a few days, and his rival would fall straight into Felix's web, leading only to humiliation. What a delight.

A spring in his step, Oxbrow bounded up onto his toes as he approached Natalya's chamber. He should have an hour at least before her morning syringe, carefully administered by the poisoner, ran out.

The guards outside her door straightened at his approach. "My lord—"

Oxbrow raised a hand, silencing the protest of whichever of the four had spoken. "Please, be at ease. I think I can handle one sedated fae." There had been an incident during Natalya's second escape attempt where she had broken the golden bindings that suppressed her blades from appearing. The faulty chains had cost him two of his best guards and had nearly demanded his life as well.

He withdrew a silver key from his pocket, leaving the golden key hidden away, and unlocked the door.

A soft rattle of metal upon metal sounded as he turned the handle. The bound fae shifting in her sleep.

He swung open the door. And a square of iron came flying toward his head.

"Aargh!" Oxbrow cried out as the iron struck his forehead, instantly splitting his skin and blinding him with his own blood. He stumbled back as the guards outside cried their alarm.

Through his swaying vision, Natalya hunched in the

center of the room, the chain she'd loosened from the wall befouled with his blood.

She yanked the chain back as the guards stormed in behind him, jostling Oxbrow in their fervor to subdue the fae.

Natalya screamed and struck one of the guards in the shoulder with her improvised weapon. It wrapped around him and hit a second in the head. He stumbled to the side away from her.

"You're just as bad as Silas!" Oxbrow screeched, spittle flying from his lips as he tried to staunch the bleeding from his head.

He glared past the fae who was kicking and clawing at the guards to the gaping hole in the wall where her chains had been affixed. She'd worked one of the nonmagical bindings loose and struck him with a fixture of his own house.

"Why I—" Oxbrow stopped short at the look in her eyes, a wild, glowing fervor. Three of the guards had finally managed to restrain her. The fourth had rushed to the apothecary case and hurried to her side, syringe in hand.

"Give her all of it!" Felix ordered. It would keep her for at least two of the three days, and then he'd have to convey her to the capital.

She struggled and sent two of the guards stumbling back, but they eventually succeeded.

Felix slumped to the floor as the guards eased the fae onto her mat. The sight of dried blood on his wrist was making him woozy. "Straight into my web," he murmured to himself, the words having lost their spark.

He'd see that the fae paid yet again for her rebellion. Both she and Graveston would be sorry before the end.

GET READY FOR REVENGE...

Natalya's journey continues in *Phantom, Heir of Lilith* book one where the Suzerain Piper foresaw crosses Natalya's path... though he's far from the charming nobleman Piper envisioned for her sister.

Far more dangerous, to be exact.

With the emerald necklace fastened to Natalya's throat, she becomes a pawn in a deadly game of courtly intrigue, secret identities, and star-crossed temptation.

Will Natalya be able to keep her promise to Piper? Or will Oxbrow's plans win out over her and Lord Silas Graveston in the end?

PHANTOM: HEIR OF LILITH BOOK ONE

His enemy's courtesan. Her only chance of escape.

A SECRET ASSASSIN

As war threatens to return to Draykemire and tensions between the courtier and noble classes grow, nobleman-by-day assassin-by-night Lord Silas Graveston has a choice to make—Ignore the insult to his family strutting about the queen's palace on the arm of his enemy or endanger his recent promotion as the public right-hand of his duke.

A CAPTIVE FAE

The provocation—a stolen emerald necklace—and the fae who wears it are both more than they appear. The necklace bears layered enchantments tantamount to a curse, and the fae cloaks herself in as many secrets as Silas himself.

Her name is Natalya Slipshayde, and she's come to the court for a single purpose. Revenge.

A MISSING HEIR

Neither Silas nor Natalya realize that they're tangled in forces far greater than treacherous courtly wiles and personal vendettas. There's a battle for the future of Draykemire being waged behind the whispers of the court. And at the center of that battle, the search for a missing fae heir who's the key to the future of both the kingdom and her world.

Natalya's adventure continues in Phantom. The queen will be expecting you.

If you loved the action and intrigue of *Promise* and you're craving even more magic, there are more high fantasy adventures to be had! In the age that follows the fall of Eldura, a cruel nobleman hatches a forced marriage plot for his half-elven stepdaughter who carries hidden magic. Her quest of destiny begins in *Buried Heroes*.

Find more adventure, enchantment, and dangers galore in the first novel in the *Age of Azuria* high fantasy series. **Get your copy today!**

A RUNAWAY NOBLEWOMAN. A CURSED WARRIOR. AND THE QUEST TO SAVE THEIR WORLD.

Buried Heroes is an epic fantasy adventure filled with magic and destiny with a slow-burn romance subplot.

Step into a world of forgotten kingdoms, ancient relics, and a prophecy that will change everything. If you love found family, reluctant heroes, and forbidden magic, then continue your fantasy adventure with Buried Heroes today!

Curious about a different magical necklace and how it, too, exerted its pull over the future of this magical world? Like the events of *Promise* and *Phantom*, this story involves a forbidden romance at the Amastacia family's seaside estate . . . Find out more by visiting beth ballbooks.com/aurora to join my newsletter and get a free copy of *Aurora*, the prequel novella for the *Age of Azuria* series!

The battle for an age begins more simply than one might think—an elven diplomat, a human noblewoman, and the forbidden love that would change their world, forever.

Elven diplomat Dorric Themear has experienced the giddy flutterings of new love before. But not like this. Behind the sapphire eyes of Lady Emelyee Amastacia lies a long-awaited destiny that neither of them can sense or stop.

However, forces darker than Emelyee's husband are prepared to stand in their way.

Close on the couple's heels, Ridel, one of Lucien's most trusted servants, is less than enthused about her assignment to watch the would-be lovers. If only her master had been visionary enough to see that a child cannot result if the parents are dead. She'll do her best to comply with his orders to observe and to wait—at least for now.

Although Dorric and Emelyee do not suspect the role they play in the larger story of Azuria, they have a secret protector lingering in the shadows, preparing for precisely this moment. High in the Frostmaw Mountains, Yvayne has seen the signs of the turning of the age before. This time, with the proper intervention, she and the druids can make their play for Azuria.

In this prequel novella for the *Age of Azuria* high fantasy series, competing forces converge in a battle for the future of their world—a future that hangs upon the return of a long-awaited soul. And, of course, on Dorric's ability to woo the human noblewoman whose affections lie beyond his reach.

Visit bethballbooks.com/aurora for a free copy of *Aurora*, the prequel novella for the *Age of Azuria* series, and find out where Iellieth's story truly began!

You'll find other exclusive stories as part of the Circle of Story, my newsletter community for all the latest book news and update. Visit the link above to join!

JOURNEY DEEPER INTO ELDURA

For character art reveals, fantasy map deep-dives, and all the latest happenings in Eldura, visit bethballbooks.com/join to be part of my newsletter community, the Circle of Story.

And finally, for special editions and exclusive covers, visit bethballbooks.shop.

About the Author

Beth Ball is a weaver of words and worlds spinning stories of druidic magic and the power of nature that span the epic fantasy realms of Azuria and Eldura. If you enjoy lyrical tales of action and adventure, dragons, werewolves, fae, wily foxes, and more, then grab your enchanted amulet, flaming longsword, poisoned dagger, or other mystical accessory of choice, and let's start our adventure!

You can find more of Beth's work and the legends of Azuria and Eldura at bethballbooks.com. And if you're looking for playable, immersive adventures in Azuria, visit groveguardianpress.com.

GLOSSARY

The following glossary entries may contain light spoilers for the worldbuilding and characters of Promise. For a more comprehensive list alongside lore and cross-series interconnections, visit bethballbooks.com/glossary.

WORLDS & PLANES

Planes of Life, *three interconnected planes,* Eldura, Shadowlands, and Brightlands
Negative Planes, origin planes of the negata
Elemental Planes, one for each element, ruled over by and encompassing the power of each elemental titan
Astralei, spirit plane
Eldura, central world of the planes of life, made up of kingdoms and great cities including the kingdom of Draykemire
Shadowlands, lower world of the planes of life, including the sprawling kingdom of Verrain

Kingdoms

Draykemire, kingdom ruled by Queen Alsea; once ruled by dragons until they were overthrown by the Orbaskier family line
Verrain, neighboring kingdom nearest to Draykemire through the portals between Eldura and the Shadowlands
Neverune, an ancient name for the region that now holds Draykemire, Respite, and Vestige

Court of Draykemire

Queen Alsea, ruler of Draykemire, regent of Madrogas
Duke Whitaker, Queen Alsea's brother, regent of Hillearst
Duke Heinrik, Queen Alsea's brother, regent of the Serra Valley

Class Structure of Draykemire

Queen/King
Duke, Duchess, and Regent
Earl/Countess
Viscount/Viscountess
Lord/Lady
Nobility
Courtier class (courtesan, consort)
Knighthood

Priestesses/Priests
Merchants/Traders, Artisans
Any and all others would fall beneath this class structure

ELEMENTAL TITANS

Gaia, titan of earth
Ignis, titan of fire
Atamos, titan of air
Ilona, titan of light
Thalyssa, titan of water
Nyx, titan of darkness
Verdigris, titan of nature, *destroyed and transformed into the three planes of life*
Izadra, titan of space, *destroyed and transformed into the spirit plane, Astralei*

DEITIES

Alessandra, "the dark goddess"
Gwyneth, goddess of autumn and the harvest
Rasvana, creator goddess of dragons

FOLKLORIC HEROES

Lilith, revolutionary figure for the Shadowlands fae
Vengeance, hero of the negata who helped to free them from their homeland in the Negative Planes
Hugh & Lilia, a Lycan and a fae, respectively; heroes

before the Fall of the First Age who sacrificed their love to save their peoples

MAGES AND MAGIC-CASTERS

Alchemists
Bellemancers
Biomancers
Druids
Elemental casters, usually specialize in individual elements: windspeakers [air], lightbringers [light], earthshapers [earth], aquabearers [water], firemancers [fire], shadowweavers [darkness]
Necromancers
Priestesses/priests, usually connected to a deity or titan